Director of the Tours

Misadventures of a Tour Director in Alaska

Fred Colvin

Since 1978

PO Box 221974 Anchorage, Alaska 99522-1974
books@publicationconsultants.com
www.publicationconsultants.com

ISBN 978-1-59433-198-5
eBook ISBN 978-1-59433-207-4
Library of Congress Catalog Card Number: 2011921686

Manufactured in the United States of America.

To our children - Randall, Tobias, and Christina.

Contents

The following stories are from adventures from aboard cruise ships.

Preface

Alaska has been my home for the past 34 years. Since becoming a tour director 10 summers ago, I have shown more than 6,000 tourists from every U.S. state and Canadian province, plus several dozen countries, around our glorious state. With this many people involved in joining me on land tours, interesting and sometimes odd occurrences are bound to take place. I have always enjoyed reporting on the happenings in my life, and now I wish to share these touring experiences with you.

Alaska has a certain unexplainable magic to some people, whom have chosen to visit us and are able to open their eyes enough to see and appreciate it. Hopefully, through these stories, I have been able to transfer some of that Alaska magic to your inner self.

Evil Arm

This was my first tour of the second season. Our guests flew into Fairbanks, then took the train to Denali Park, and finally motor coached down to Seward—after five days of Alaska tourism bliss.

I knew that financially, I had to do this job for a second season, but I wasn't quite sure I was ready emotionally. I had just finished a reasonably steady 14 weeks of substitute teaching in the Alaska native villages of Holy Cross and Nondalton only a few weeks before.

I now sat on our train car trying to refashion that obsequious smile that goes with this business and would hide my efforts to process the incredibly bizarre reality of the rural Alaska experience that I had just finished witnessing.

"Our beautiful train cars were built in Fort Lupton, Colorado for 2.2 million dollars each. They are the longest, tallest, and, some say, most luxurious train cars in the world!"

This was Mary, the host guide on this train leg of our tour. Mary was a chunky, 40-something woman about five foot ten in height.

I had been warned about her already, that she was different. I was keeping an eye on her and already was getting peeved, because she held the microphone a millimeter from her mouth and when she said something that she thought was funny, she would laugh in a deep guffaw and not move the microphone. I was getting some uncomfortable looks from some of my guests.

It was my job to work on paperwork and mingle during the three to four hours we would be traveling between Fairbanks and Denali National Park. The guests would also be served a reasonably priced breakfast. I always prefaced breakfast as 'reasonably priced' because most of our guests thought that since the food on board their cruise ship was included in their tour package, ipso-facto, it would be free on the land portion also.

"Our mixologist will be Natalie. Stand up Natalie. Oh! She is standing up! Ha, ha, ha, ha, ha."

Natalie was about eight inches shorter than Mary Jo and I could tell by her grimace that Mary Jo and she would be having words later.

"She'll fix you coffee, hot chocolate, and some people even start their day with Bloody Marys.

This was going to be a long morning. I could feel it in my bones, that were presently being shook by the horse laughter going through the microphone. This first group of 36 people seemed tame enough. The first two weeks and the last two weeks of the tourism season in Alaska is generally made up of guests whom have gotten great discounts. They usually get to see the snow from the previous winter in May and the snow from the impending winter in September. These discounted groups also require a bit of coaxing to go on any land excursions that would cost them money. Thus, I need to be actively creative in my nightly notes under their doors, so I won't get stiffed at the end of our time together. I learned last season that the term being stiffed refers to people who choose not to tip you. I love words, so I often wonder why stiff would have anything to do with cheap people.

"Do all of you see the four inch step-up to your seats? Well, that step down becomes four feet if you forget it's there—and you might accidentally feel up your neighbors as you fall. Ha, ha, ha, ha, ha."

That was enough. I stood up and approached Mary. I could see a nervous look on her face as I approached her.

"May I talk with you." I asked and we stepped a few steps down the staircase that led to the kitchen.

"Hi Mary," I introduced myself and I felt her enormous breasts press against me.

"Oh Fred, I've heard so much about you. How am I doing? This is my first trip of the season," she seemed genuinely excited.

Its funny how we men are. I was prepared to give her a scathing review, but when pressed against her womanhood, instead I simply said, "You're doing great, but, if you could hold the mike away from your mouth a little further, everyone could understand you better."

"Oh thanks," she kissed me on the cheek, "I know we're going to work great together this season."

I turned and went back to my seat.

The train crew had the toughest job of anyone in our company. Last year, the most turnover of employees, occurred on the train. They start in Anchorage at 7:30 in the morning fixing breakfast to 80 people as we travel north to Talkeetna. Then, a new 80 passengers get on board for lunch, which is served on the way to Denali Park. Finally a group gets on for dinner which is served on the way to Fairbanks. The six member crew are carted to an apartment in Fairbanks, where they generally arrive by 10 PM if there had been no delays. Then, they are to be at the train station by 7 AM the next morning for the ride back to Anchorage.

One of the main problems with the train job is finding crew members whom are compatible. Being constantly busy and working in such close proximity to one another makes the job similar to being under the ice for several months in the submarine Nautilus. Each week, I would find new faces on the five different crews that rotated shifts on the two train cars going north and two going south. Listening to their petty squabbles becomes part of the rituals of this job.

"I will now begin rotating people downstairs for breakfast. We have table space for 36 people at each setting. But, I promise that all of you will get to eat our scrumptious breakfast—hours before we roll into Denali Park!"

Mary really wasn't that bad of a host guide—It was simply her first trip and her nerves had taken over. It always surprises me that people, including myself, allow the new position of authority they attain to lead them out of their true identity and into a role they *think* others want them to be. I guess it easy for me to say this now, from my viewing box of 61 years into this game.

"Fred," I looked up from my pondering to see Mr. Longley. I pegged his name right off because he had a pronounced long face. "I know that we have had a lot of fun so far. But I, we have a serious problem."

His face furrowed in deep lines of worry and concern. I couldn't help but wonder at what age he began to cultivate those now fully mature frown creases.

"Sit down Mr. Longley," I scooted over. "What is the problem?"

"Well," Longley leaned over and whispered, "Everyone seemed so nice in our group. But I'm afraid," he leaned his head closer to my ear, "I believe that we have a thief on board."

I smiled inwardly.

"What's happened?" I asked. Sounding somewhat like Detective Clueso in the Peter Sellers movies.

"My wife is missing her gold bracelet." The whispering continued, "It wasn't any ordinary bracelet."

"Hoo so?" I had now become Sellers and had puckered my lips up looking very concerned—while inwardly trying not to smile as I remembered my friend Phil from my old *Pronto Pup Days* and how any reference to Sellers would send him into parody and infectious fits of laughter that quickly had all around him affected.

"What?" Longley looked at me strangely.

"Hoo is the brooslet diffrent?" I said keeping a straight face.

"There are ten diamonds on it and it is worth five figures," Longley now moved away, as I think he felt that I wasn't reacting as he expected.

"Ohhh…"

"What are you going to do?" Longley now looked angry.

I snapped myself out of my Seller's role. (Tips were now in jeopardy.) I explained to him that people often feel that they have lost items on the train and then find them where they had left them on the motor coach when they get to their destination. I also assured him that I would have Mary announce to everyone to really look around their seats, once we begin disembarking.

Longley wandered back to his seat.

I really doubted that the bracelet had been stolen. But, I decided to make a walking pass through the train car to see if I could try and deduce if any couple had a larcenous look to them. I really wished I had a hat like Peter Sellers used to wear. When I passed Longley, he secretly gave me a thumbs up. He knew what I was up to. After 10 or 15 minutes of mingling, I returned to my seat, reasonably convinced that these 18 couples had not chosen to come to Alaska to propagate a diamond heist.

"Off to your right you will see the top secret radar towers from the Clear Air Force Base. Someone thought they were giant bug zappers that kill our state bird—the mosquito! Ha, ha, ha, ha, ha."

"Fred," It was Longley again. He sat beside me. "My wife found her bracelet," Longley said reassuringly and touched my arm.

"Where was it," I asked, somewhat relieved.

"It was on her other arm," Longley said and shook his head to the negative as he walked away.

I sat there stunned. I turned to see Mrs. Longley holding up that other arm and pointing to the bracelet.

This was my first tour of the second season, and I had forgotten about the nuances of this job.

Damn that other arm! That evil other arm—I smiled.

Seeing Whales

It had been raining for two or three weeks, fairly constantly. I was becoming reasonably bored with the number of 60-some-things" approaching me and squinching up their faces with a certain desperation that screamed from their inner-core that possibly, just possibly, the thousands of dollars that they had laid out for this dream vacation up north may have been poorly invested.

"Do you think the weather is going to change?"

I looked to see the retired professor pleadingly wishing I could bring him sunshine by asking a question whose intellectual answer lay somewhere between Big Bird and Mr. Rogers. I gave him a look that should have made him walk away—but he didn't.

"No, really. What's the weather forecast? "

I pumped myself up, like the guy who sells rotisserie grills 24 hours a day on infomercials, and in my most ingenuous voice; "Oh, we Alaskans simply wake up, stick our heads out the window, and say, 'Well, this is our weather for today.'" That usually shuts them up for a bit.

This day offered new environs. Tour #2 was one I had not been assigned before. I picked them up in Anchorage on Wednesday and we had made our way down to Seward. It had seemed to be a fairly tame group with only the ex-professor and an ex-nun being the catalysts for meaningless conversation, thus far.

Today, we were to go out in a small boat into Resurrection Bay, have lunch on an island, then, go further into the Pacific Ocean to try and spot killer whales.

"Hello, I'm Captain Jim and I will be your guide today." His voice sounded young coming over the loud speakers. He was up top on our 100-foot boat and his 60 or so prisoners, and myself, were huddled in the lower inside deck to escape the driving rainstorm.

"How old is Captain Jim?" I asked one of the cute young girls who were downstairs to help with the passengers.

"I think he is just 21. This is his first trip. "

I smiled.

The trip to Fox Island was fairly uneventful. We saw sea otters and puffins and the customers fought for good photo spots. I used this time to mix, which meant that I tried my hardest to act like I wanted to know more about them and listen intently as they told me lies about their lives. We always exchanged e-mail addresses and promised to write—but nobody ever does.

Anyway, Fox Island offered this buffet type lunch centered upon a fairly greasy piece of salmon, which I wondered about, since it was near the end of the season, and the salmon had been caught in May.

Everyone seemed fairly happy as we boarded The Explorer, 45 minutes later. "All aboard everyone! This is Captain Jim. Let's go see some whales."

I had been on this trip before, when I was an indentured servant (school teacher) many field trips occurred on this vessel. I had some inkling as to what was about to happen.

I was talking with the ex-nun when we began to notice the boat reacting to the swells in the ocean.

"Oh my, "she said "I didn't bring any Dramamine."

I smiled.

Within 10 minutes, the hum of conversation amongst the 60 passengers had become a deathly silence. I glanced around and saw that the previously pleasant looks people had, were now replaced with looks of dire seriousness.

"Sorry about the swells folk, but guess what I see? Over at the starboard—killer whales!"

The people pried themselves up with their thousand dollar investments of video equipment and pushed to the starboard side and began filming. The 20 minutes or so of filming seemed to temporarily numb them to the constant bobbing and sideways motions of the boat.

"We're off to see what else we can find!"

As they walked back to their places, I noticed that a Japanese couple hadn't budged and both had seasick bags up to their mouths. Whether the Japanese got it all started or not, I don't know. But, in the next 10 minutes, 40 of the 60 people began vomiting. Some were crawling on the floor. It was as if the 40 sick ones had entered a different reality. They looked like they thought they were going to die. My ex-nun looked particularly green. Since I thought that my tips may be at risk, I offered to help her—right as Captain Jim was speaking. "Look along the coast. There's an immature bald eagle in his nest!"

The ex-nun looked up at me and said ... "Bag the bald eagle! Tell him to take us back!"

I transferred that information to Captain Jim and we soon found calmer waters.

I decided that I liked this tour.

Rhythm on the Road

There is a rhythm to this wonderful life of ours. A cadence—a synchronicity. Have you noticed it?

The job Celia and I have—showing off this picturesque North Land to 40 or so guests each week, occasionally brings this rhythm to our attention. Allow me to give you an example from last week.

Celia, Jesse, and I were on a tour that required that we get up early on a Wednesday morning to see off our guests on a 55-mile trip into Denali National Park. The 131 guests had been divided onto three park buses that would leave from our hotel at 6:50 AM, 7:10 AM, and 7:30 AM—sounds easy.

6:30 AM: The phone rings and Celia answers it—she talks in a concerned manner to one of her guests and then hangs up shaking her head. It seems that a woman's 19-year-old daughter was having an adverse effect to some sinus medication she had been taking and the woman wanted to get her to a hospital. She had gone to a local clinic the day before, but wasn't happy with their treatment. The girl was missing her boyfriend and the woman was recently divorced. Celia knew their illness was multi-dimensional. In any event, the two would not be going on the 7:30 AM trip into the park.

7:10 AM: I have handed out all but two of my Tundra Wilderness Tour tickets and don't see two missing guests. So, I head to the lobby to phone their room while my other 38 guests load onto the 7:10 bus. The missing couple is a sweet pair of 77-year-olds whom reminded me of my recently deceased parents. I find out that they have overslept, but will try to get down to the bus in 10 minutes. "If we're not there'" Ruth's shaking voice said," let the bus go."

7:15 AM: I returned to the bus and find Jesse standing beside my bus with two of his guests. There had been a rather unpleasant altercation on his bus, the 6:50 AM bus. A mentally challenged, obese woman had refused to allow anyone to sit beside her. This rude reality disallowed the couple now standing before me from entering their full bus. I thought about simply saying no, since I felt sure that my older couple would be coming soon, but instead I told them that we'd wait until 7:20 AM and then the other couple could take the seats. This was my 97th tour and I somehow felt that things would work out.

7:21 AM: I had just watched Jesse's couple take the last two seats on my 7:10 AM bus, when my older couple, the Rinne's, came hustling out of the hotel's doorway. Both sets of eyes were filled with tears, as they watched the bus pull away. My heart sank as Ruth told me that the main reason they had come to Alaska was to see the grizzly bears in Denali Park, but I still felt that things might work out. I then spotted Celia, who had handed out all but two of her tickets. Her bus was running late. I suddenly remembered the early morning phone call.

Celia and I introduced the Rinnes to two other couples, Celia had deemed as kind-hearted and could watch out for my older couple, and they all eventually went on their way.

3:30PM: When the bus pulled up in front of the hotel eight hours later, a tired but excited Ruth and Ray Rinne came up to me. They had seen 10 grizzly bears, countless caribou, a wolf, but most importantly Ruth shared with me—they had made four new friends.

Ruth leaned forward and kissed me on the cheek, "You made this happen," she said with a smile.

I smiled back, knowing that I had little to do with it. It had happened as it was supposed to have happened. A rhythm of life—allowed expression.

This photo was taken from the top of Mt. Healy in Denali Park. The zig-zaggy road in the distance, on the right, leads up to the hotel where the Rinnes were staying.

Man Servant

It was the last tour of the season and I was hoping to get bumped off of the TWT. (Tundra Wildlife Tour, a 55 or 64 mile trip into Denali National Park.) It wasn't that I didn't enjoy it, but I noticed who the driver was and I wasn't sure that my now fragile psychology could handle another seven hour trip with this woman.

"Hi Fred," she said and I waited for the next words that might save me from this destiny, but they didn't come, "I have some front seats blocked off for some Princess guests that I have to pick up, but there should be a seat for you in the back."

When I got to the back, I saw that there was one open set of seats above the hump where the back tire was, and one open seat beside a 300 pound plus guest who was already shoving potato chips down his gullet. I chose the hump.

Down the switch backs from the Grande Denali Hotel we went. I sighed because my knees were already a few inches from my face, after hitting a couple of bumps. This trip was going to be a test. I sensed it.

The bus pulled up in front of the Princess Hotel and people filed on, filling in the saved seats the driver had cordoned off. I could have a full set of two seats to myself—I sighed. Then the driver hit the brakes and opened the door. There entered two women in full Indian garb. I instantly labeled them Indira and the Ugly One.

Indira chose to sit beside me and put her mother beside the heavy set man, now covered in potato chip crumbs.

There was an instant musty odor and I almost gagged. "I'll move over with that man, if you'd like to sit with your mother?" I offered realizing I had made a tactical error. I knew the obese man now to be a pleasant guy and probably much less of a psychological challenge than this woman might be.

"Who are you?" Indira demanded and all of my guests noticed the scorn in her voice.

I explained that I was a tour director for 42 guests on this bus and that I had to accompany them on this trip into the park. I then reissued my request that she move to be with her mother.

"Oh no, my mother driving me crazy. I stay with you. You be my man servant."

'Holy ....,' I thought to myself as we hit another bump and I fell into her musty smelling clothes. My guests were all smiling at me—enjoying fully the predicament I had gotten myself into.

"Did you know that Denali National Park is the same size as the state of Massachusetts?" the driver began her monotonous dialog that somewhere after the second hour usually made me want to blow my brains out. Add to this, my new role as a man servant for Indira and this looked to be quite a final TWT.

I found out that her husband and father chose not to come. "I think I am getting on their nerves," she said and then laughed a very loud laugh that bordered between maniacal and staged.

Now, my guests were giggling. I decided to keep her talking and asked her questions about Calcutta. It was obvious that she was from money and was used to being waited on.

"That woman driving is boring. You tell me about this place. You my personal man servant." She then leaned her shoulder toward me in an endearing fashion and it seemed that the red dot between her eyes was pulsating.

I tried to explain to her about why we weren't seeing very many animals. Then, she would lean back to her mother, who evidently didn't speak much English, and say something in her native language in a terse way and the woman would scream something back. The obese man sitting beside the Ugly One looked quite frightened. Her ugliness stemmed from the fact that her darkened face had wrinkles that went directions that they shouldn't have, and seemed to point to the fact that, just maybe this woman had never smiled in her life.

"Did you know that Dall sheep stand up on those high ridges for the whole year?"

We were looking at two very far away white dots that the driver reassured us were dall sheep. Indira was leaning against me looking through some cheap binoculars and I could feel her breasts through her silk outer garments. I thought I was starting to fall for my little musty smelling, Calcutta concubine when she screamed in disdain. "I see no sheep! I see no sheep!"

The hours passed slowly. I saw one of our other tour directors, Jack, sleeping on another bus. He had the entire back of that bus to himself. Where is the justice in my world?

When it came time to eat our snack box, of course, Indira and the Ugly One could not eat since it was not a vegetarian meal.

So, I watched Indira pull out a lettuce sandwich and begin squeezing packets of mustard onto the lettuce. The trouble being that I sat nearly in her lap on a very bumpy part of the gravel road and was wearing light brown pants. I wondered to myself, *how much worse could this experience get?*

I tried to sleep.

"Animals! Animals!"

I awoke to Indira leaning against me yelling because a moose was standing 100 yards away.

"Shhhh" the driver tried to calm Indira and the Ugly One who was now also pressed up against me. I ended up taking photographs for both of them, and thought briefly about rubbing the two red dots from their foreheads. Like Edgar Allen Poe's eye in *The Tell Tale Heart*, the red dots were starting to get to me. I somehow found patience to endure the rest of this trip.

A photo that Indira got of the sheep using her telephoto lens.

When the two Indian ladies were dropped off at the Princess Hotel, my guests let me have it—telling me that they had never enjoyed watching someone else's misery as much as they did watching mine.

The next season we weren't required to go on the TWTs—but this year I may once again be called into my man servant role.

Love Lost

This is a tour that I didn't get to do this year, but last year it served as an awakening for me. On tour #8, the customers come off of their cruise ship in Seward, where I meet them. We then travel by motor coach to spend the night in Anchorage. What follows is three legs of being on the train, before they fly home from Fairbanks.

This is a fairly insecure tour for the motor coach drivers. They realize that the three hour trip from Seward to Anchorage is their only chance to convince the 36 customers that they are, beyond a shadow of anyone's doubt, the most proficient, witty, and safe drivers to walk the  planet. The rest of the trip they simply drive the customer's luggage to the hotels, while the customers and I have leisurely train rides between locations. This convincing will of course result in major tips, if they can pull this ruse off.

This aspect of Tour #8 really has little to do with the story I want to tell you. But, I just can't leave out the reality of my driver on this tour. My driver was Elmo.

Elmo was an odd looking little 74-year-old man who worked as a substitute school bus driver in the off season. Elmo was also a cowboy. Well, actually, he only dressed like a cowboy. He really only started doing this when he and his wife began square dancing a dozen years or so back.

Now, don't let me mislead you. I kind of liked Elmo. I made my fourth-graders square dance for many years, just for the sheer enjoyment of seeing the children hate/love holding hands for the first time. Also, he drove the brand new $450,000 Prevost Motor coaches at maximum speed at all times. I would steal glances at the customers being thrown to and fro and smile to myself, as we all held on for dear life.

It's Elmo's night-time habits that are forcing me to bring him into this story. The first year of this touring company was sort of an experiment. The cruise line had never been involved with the land portion of Alaska before. So, they really didn't know how the interpersonal dynamics of this boat and pony show would work. So, this first year, drivers and tour directors many times stayed in the same hotel rooms together. This turned out not to work, because tour directors were generally phoned in their rooms all hours of the night by insecure customers and the drivers didn't like that.

On this tour, I didn't have to room with Elmo. We were traveling with 35 guests in another motor coach and their driver Deron was with tour director Dot. Dot and I lucked out with rooms of our own, but Deron and Elmo had to share rooms.

I assure you that Deron had his own peculiarities. But, that will have to be another story.

It was through Deron's report that we learned that Elmo, besides being an excellent square dancer and Indianapolis 500 motor coach driver, was a practicing nudist—which isn't easy to do in Alaska. It seems that Elmo would immediately strip down when he got into his room and wear only his cowboy hat and boots.

Deron would come whimpering to my room and I would let him stay with me. He and I became great friends that first year, all because of Elmo's evident pride in the skin portion of his being. Deron didn't return for the second season and I wondered if it was Elmo's doing. Anyway, to get back to the reason I bring Tour #8 to the forefront.

The first three or four weeks that I began as a tour director last year were tense. Having a classroom of children was totally different than being in charge of a motor coach filled with older adults—or so I thought it would be. Then at a point while we were waiting for the train in Talkeetna to pick us up and take us on to Denali Park, something happened that made this job a gift, rather than a test.

I had a group of nested pairs. I call them this because there were no groups traveling together, only couples. This tends to be a challenge because the couples have trouble interacting. When there are groups of six or more traveling together, there exists a hierarchy amongst them that continuously creates some type of humor—and generally fun. But this group was a *yawner*. I had even tried the game *Two truths and a lie* with them on the way to Anchorage and the most exciting thing that we discovered was that one woman had danced with Lawrence Welk.

As I look back, I realize that I was trying too hard to be the perfect tour guide. This was my 4th or 5th group and I had developed this pattern of delivering information about Alaska in a somewhat clinical manner and although people seemed to enjoy their land tours with me, I was beginning to feel that this was basically just a very time consuming job.

I had been told that the train would be at least 30 minutes late, so I put my *Alaska Grizzlies* videotape into the VCR, that broadcasted over five strategically placed TV monitors in the motor coach, and sat back. It was a beautiful day and I encouraged people to get off the motor coach and walk around if they wanted, and several people did. But, under no circumstance were they to cross the yellow line. The two Gomers that ran this little train station in the summers had obviously gone to the Barney Fife school of self-importance and would begin yelling when one person's toe would cross the yellow line toward the train tracks.

Personally, I had no problems with the yellow line. Having grown up in Decatur, Illinois, I had been subjected to hours of train/car mutilation movies in our health classes in Stephen Decatur High School. Even though the top speed of our Alaska Railroad passenger cars is around 45 miles per hour, I don't mess with them.

After about 10 minutes of the grizzly movie, I noticed one of my female passengers standing very close to the yellow line, leaning against a chain barrier that Gomer #1 had proudly put up the week before. She seemed sad as she stood a good 50 feet from the main group of people who were excitedly preparing their tripods for an action shot of the train, which was still 20 minutes away.

Wishing to be the perfect tour director I exited the motor coach and approached her. As I stepped up to her, I noticed a tear streaked face. Before disembarking the motor coach, I glanced at her husband, who was laughing too hysterically at the grizzlies scratching their backs on a road sign in Denali Park. He had to weigh in at 350 pounds and here I stood beside a woman that couldn't be more than a third of his size. "Is there something wrong?" I asked and I suddenly remembered her name to be Evelyn.

"Oh, I'm sorry," she jumped, seeming embarrassed, "I didn't see you coming."

I stood there and we were both quiet for a while. A small, yellow plane took off from a field a hundred or so yards from the yellow line, and we watched it roar into the distance.

"Would you mind if I told you a story, Fred?" Evelyn said as it became quiet again and she wiped the tears from her face.

It wasn't the manner of her request that suddenly had my heart beating fast, it was her touch. When she made the query, she reached over and softly clasped my forearm. I have always felt that separate dimensions exist through our senses and that hypothesis was once again being realized here. "Please do," I responded looking at this petite woman, who was probably in her 70s, yet her ageless blue eyes seemed to be piercing a hole through me.

"When I was in my early 20s," Evelyn began, "I fell in love with this man who was eight years older than me," she hesitated as a couple walked past us complaining that the train was going to be late.

I sighed, suddenly caring nothing about the present situation. I simply wanted to hear more from Evelyn.

"My parents weren't happy about our age difference, but they could see how much in love I was with Robert. Fred, this was a time so different from now, but love knows no society or time restrictions. When were you born, Fred?"

"1949," I responded.

"It was 1945 and 46 when this took place. I am Catholic and Robert wasn't, and back in those days, marriage between religions was simply out of the question. I kept this fact from my parents as long as I could."

"What happened?" I asked. I saw Evelyn stare off in the distance.

"When it became obvious to both of us that my family would never accept our relationship, we simply stopped seeing each other. Robert moved to California and I began dating other men."

"May I ask why you are so sad right now?"

Evelyn reached into her purse and pulled out a cell phone.

"This is the reason. My best friend in Indianapolis left a message on here that Robert passed away last night."

"Weren't there any opportunities later on in your lives for you two to get together?"

"Robert married and had three children and I found a wonderful man with whom I was married to for 38 years and we also had three wonderful children. Fate did seem to offer us another chance. His wife died a year before I lost Jeffrey. I made an effort to go and see him, but there were already several ladies with eyes toward him. Robert was always so handsome." Evelyn made a wistful smile.

The next thing that Evelyn said to me will always stay with me.

"You know Fred. People are always so quick to announce that they have 'fallen out of love' with someone. But, I feel that once you love someone—that love is always with you. People only delude themselves. I loved Robert all of my life. I will miss the fact that his warm heart is not beating somewhere on this beautiful planet." she said and squeezed my arm a little tighter.

My eyes began watering and Evelyn leaned over and gave me a kiss on the cheek.

"You are very sweet to let this old lady tell you her story."

"How long have you and the gentleman on the motor coach been together?" I asked, still a bit shaken.

"Oh Dan? He and I are not married. He lost his wife recently and they had this trip to Alaska planned years in advance. I told him I would accompany him and I'm glad I did. I am getting to see this beautiful state and I am getting to know you."

The train suddenly appeared and we were shaken from the trance Evelyn's story had created. Evelyn walked to be with Dan as we boarded our train heading North.

Time took on nonlinear dimensions the rest of that day for me. My breathing seemed at much more of a controlled cadence. Considering her thoughts about love, allowed me reflection to the handful of girls who had carved out a portion of my heart. Time stops when you are in love. People who don't believe in time travel weren't paying attention when they were in love. The rest of life is simply props when you're inside love's wonderful glow.

Whether it was a combination of Evelyn's touch and presence or maybe it was simply a moment I needed to experience. I will never pretend to understand this incredible life we are given. I do know that I was pulled into a timeless moment with this woman I truly didn't even know.

Since that moment, I became a different tour director. I did, as I had learned to do as a school teacher, to wait until I had met each group before a strategy could be devised as to how our time together would be spent. I have 26 years of experiences in Alaska and I have found that some groups pull out memories and others don't. My comfort level remains steady and I remain true to each group's chemistry.

There have been a few other people, since Evelyn, who have opened up their hearts to me.

My being here to listen is part of the job—part of the life.

IRS Agent

It had started raining three days earlier. I stood in the lobby of the hotel in Talkeetna and noticed many of the 36 souls with whom I had accompanied from Anchorage that morning, gazing forlornly out of the window at where Mt. McKinley should be. Instead, a steady rainfall and fog bank gave them a view barely a hundred yards from the window. They all seemed to glance at me and shake their heads. Oh yeah—It was my really all my fault!

It was late in the season, so my obsequious nature was running thin. But, I did explain that only 30% of the visitors to Talkeetna get to view the mountain, and that Talkeetna still was a quirky little town to explore.

Okay, I had done my duty. Now it was my time to relax and have a bite to eat. I wandered into the bar/restaurant and spied two other tour directors. I could act like I didn't see them, and back out quickly. One of the toughest parts of this tour directing job is dealing with the different levels of psychosis represented by my peers.

"Fred. Join us." it was Kate who intercepted my retreat.

"Sure," I pulled a barstool up to the small round table. I liked Kate who was from Colorado and recovering from a divorce six years earlier. I am learning that women never stop hating the men that do them wrong.

"Fred, this is Jackie," We shook hands." I vaguely remembered her. She seemed a bit too serious acting, so I had kept a distance. Now I was stuck here for dinner. She had a sweet smile, but her eye teeth were a little too pronounced for my liking.

"Fred and I have worked three weeks together this summer," Kate offered, "He really is a riot."

Okay, that comment sealed it. I would do the quick in and out method one CC and water. Skip dinner and have dessert—then off to the safety of my room.

Jackie giggled and waited for me to say something witty.

I ordered my drink as two huge orders of French fries smothered in gravy came. "I like women who aren't worried about their cholesterol count," I said and got two guarded giggles.

It was then that I noticed an older lady motioning me from the doorway. She may have been one of my group. I had to respond. Sometimes I can't recognize faces three days later. Names and faces just isn't high on my ability chart. "Excuse me girls," I got up and approached the lady.

"Fred, we have a problem," she said. I saw her husband and I knew that she was with my group. Her husband looked just like Jim Backus or Mr. Magoo. So, to my mind she was Mrs. Magoo.

"What's the problem?" I gave my best concerned look.

"Our son Richard went jogging three hours ago, and he hasn't returned," Mrs. Magoo was wringing her hands and Mr. Magoo was mumbling something incomprehensible to himself.

When I had met Magoo at the hotel in Anchorage, he had given me a hint that he just may be trouble.

Flashback—In Anchorage the night before.

"I used to teach," Magoo began when he found out that I was a retired teacher, "to make a long story short…." then began 20 straight minutes of him rambling, reasonably insanely, about the lack of discipline in today's schools and his minor role in some school in Southern California. "I brought my son up here for a break from his high-stress job. He handles corporate cases with the IRS."

"Tell him that I'm a retired teacher and I keep all of my receipts in a shoe box.," I tried to muse with Magoo—Magoo didn't laugh.

"My wife and I brought him up here to meet women. All he ever does is drink beer and watch football on his cable TV—he's 36 and should be interested in women, don't you think, Fred."

Those remembrances brought me back to my two maligned faces. "I'm sure he's fine. Maybe he got just got lost on some of the trails behind the lodge. Let's see, it's 6:30. I'll finish my meal by 7, and if he hasn't shown up by then, we'll call some people," I tried to sound reassuring. After all this could be a major tips windfall.

"Are there any bears on those trail?" Mrs. Magoo's voice held a bit of a quiver—I know that I smiled a bit.

"Well, yes, both black bears and grizzlies are around ma'am, but none have been seen lately." I said, I couldn't help myself, "We can only hope that he doesn't jog past one. Running does trigger the chase and destroy instinct in bears."

I walked back to the bar, reasonably proud of how I had handled the situation. I glanced back to see the Magoo's huddled in terror.

I approached the table and saw that my two grease-baronesses had devoured around two-thirds of their gravy and fries. I quickly plotted on how to present my new-found vignette, and then sat back down.

My drink was awaiting me, so I took a healthy swig.

"Any problems?" Kate asked, with that glint in her eye that all tour directors get when they hope that one of their peers may have in any small way screwed something up. It somehow adds legitimacy to our existence.

"Possibly," I hesitated to prolong the effect.

"Well?" they both seemed to say at once and I recorded a small victory, because I briefly had stopped the intake of gravied fries down their gullets.

"I can see one, possibly even three less envelopes on Friday."

Jackie looked at Kate for a translation.

"That's Fred's way of saying tips. Tips are in the envelopes. What happened?" Kate asked with a little more force, finding less humor in my efforts for dramatic effect.

"Remember Mr. 'To make a long story short' in Anchorage." Kate nodded. She found great humor seeing me trapped in Magoo's senseless conversation. "Well, I guess his 36-year-old son went jogging three hours ago, and has not returned."

"He's probably drunk down at the Fairview Inn," Kate offered.

"No, Magoo said he had made a pass through town and there was no sight of him. A lot of things could have happened."

"Like what?" Jackie asked seeming bored.

"Last year there were bears all over the place around here. But, that's not really my guess." I took another swig of my drink and ordered my dessert, the Molehill Cake, which was this rich, dark chocolate concoction that most of the female tour directors made orgasmic sounds as they ate. I had a few problems with the name they chose for this sweet decadence because it brought back memories of my father violently striking his spade in our yard as he killed this mole that had created a most interesting design with molehills—obviously, moaning women hadn't had like experiences.

"Is this guy for real?" Jackie asked sipping a martini.

"How old are you?" I asked. "Thirty?"

"Thirty-two," she answered.

"Fred, leave her alone" Kate interrupted, "What do you think happened to the guy?"

"Think about it; 36 years old; traveling with mommy and daddy; an IRS agent who has ruined countless lives, and probably has had his heart chewed up by women for half his life. Did you notice how he wears that baseball cap down over his eyes. All school psychologists say that kids who do this are hiding something."

"What is he hiding?" Jackie offered.

"Seems obvious to me, manic depression, probably jogged up to the Susitna River in this driving rain storm and thought *what's the sense going on*? Later tonight they will be dragging the river and you know what they'll find? His pitiful body and three empty envelopes that should have been filled with fresh green bills for me on Friday!"

"You're crazy," Jackie said and Kate laughed.

They brought me my molehill cake and I noticed the girls licking the grease off of their forks as they prepared to eat a third of my delicacy—women always get away with this theft.

I checked the watch on Jackie's wrist. Ten till seven. Enough time to eat.

About halfway through the cake, or a sixth of the way through if I factored in the female-possessed forks, I decided to find out more about Jackie. "So, Jackie. Do you have any plans for the winter?" Jackie looked at Kate and hesitated.

"Is there a secret here, I'm invading?"

"No," Kate offered, "We were just talking about that though."

"I don't want to tell you Fred because you are the kind of sarcastic bum who would make fun of my plans."

"You don't even know me?" I defended myself.

"I know you well enough to realize that you have no compassion for one of your guests, who might be in peril, and your only concern is whether you'll miss out on some tips."

"That is true," I quipped, "But give me a chance. There may be more to me than you think."

She hesitated and I swallowed my last piece of the mole.

"I guess our chances of seeing each other again are pretty close to nil. Okay here goes. I want to be an actress and be in movies and television. I plan on going to Hollywood, getting an apartment, and trying to realize my dream."

"Have you acted before?" I asked, trying to sound empathetic.

"Only in my high school senior class play. But I really enjoyed doing that."

I glanced at her Mickey Mouse wrist watch. Two more minutes. I searched for the last traces of Canadian Club Whiskey amongst the ice cubes in my glass.

"Well? Aren't you going to say something rude?"

"No. I have no right to judge your dreams. We all should follow our bliss—as Joseph Campbell would say."

"Then, why are you smiling?" Kate asked

"Oh, I was just thinking how Jackie's dream is so inspiring that I may just take my summer earnings down to San Francisco, get an apartment across from a fire station, buy a half a gallon of brass polish, and daily go over to the station and polish their pole. Maybe, just maybe I could somehow become a fireman. I've always wanted to be a fireman." I said this as I was getting up and smiled at Jackie as she gave me the finger with both hands.

As I walked back into the lobby, I giggled wondering if my analogy of polishing poles was lost on Jackie.

I saw the Magoo's over at the window looking behind the lodge.

"He hasn't returned yet?"

"No," Mr. Magoo began, "I had a worker take an ATV back on those trails to see if maybe Richard got lost. He's been gone around 15 minutes." The 4-wheeler than came out of the clouds, through the trees, and stopped about 100 feet from the entrance. It was still raining hard, so I offered to go out and ask him if he had seen anything.

"Any luck?" I asked the man in the camouflage green rain gear.

"Who the hell are you?"

"Mr. Magoo sent me out here to see if you spotted his son on the trails."

Mr. Green Camouflage Rain Gear Man stepped off of the 4-wheeler and rivulets of water cascaded from his person into a larger river on the asphalt. He then spit some tobacco, not far from me. "I went on every trail there is and saw nothing. Why is anyone crazy enough to be jogging in this weather anyway?" He hesitated. "He's probably drinking down at the Fairview."

I liked this guy. I came here every week, yet had never seen him before. Talkeetna drew the strangest people. I'll have to do some research to find out which prison it was that had recently released him.

"What did he say?" Mrs. Magoo ran up to me as I reentered the lodge. Although I can understand a mother's anxiety in this situation, it still made me ponder whether she had weaned him at age 34.

"Sorry, he saw no sign of anyone."

"I got the State Troopers' number from the front desk," Magoo said heading for the phone on the wall, "I'm going to go call."

The Magoos, in a high level of stress, began punching the numbers and I noticed someone in a ball cap coming from the hallway that led to the rooms, then walking into the restaurant—could it be Magoo Jr.?

I left the distraught parents and went into the restaurant. .Kate and Jackie were still there having another drink.

It was Magoo Jr. and he was bumping into people's chairs as he now tried to get out of the restaurant.

"Hi Richard," He tried to ignore me. "Where have you been?"

"Out on the toown," he slurred and I could smell the alcohol on his breath.

"Your parents are on the phone calling the State Troopers. They have been worried sick."

"I'm okay." We made our way across the lobby and I noticed another one of my guests pointing at him.

His parents embraced him as he walked up to them. Then,

when it was obvious he was drunk, they whisked him away to their rooms. It was apparent that Magoo Junior was going to have to spend some time in Time Out.

I saw the woman who had been pointing at him was motioning for me to come over. She was the leader of this group of four couples from New Jersey, four doctors and their wives, who had bragged to me the night before that they were going on their 21st cruise together. "I am con-

A photo of the Talkeetna Alaskan Lodge on a clear day.

sidering pressing charges against that young man you just led in here." She sounded indignant.

"What did he do?"

"When we were all coming back from town on the shuttle, he got on and was so drunk he could hardly stand up and fell against me—he squeezed my right breast."

"He was so drunk that when he got off here he fell face first into a puddle," her husband laughed.

"You may want to rethink any charges. He's a hotshot for the IRS in California and is on this trip to relieve pressure. His parents told me."

There was a hesitation.

Then Mrs. Right Breast Squeezed said, "Oh, I guess there wasn't any ill intent. He was just drunk."

"I wish he would have squeezed my breasts. Howie never does," another New Jerseyite said and they all laughed.

I quickly made my way to the safety of my room.

J. & J. Restaurant

I had been warned about tour #4. Tours #3 and #4 are four day tours that involve no train portions, so the tour directors have many hours of motor coach time to educate and entertain their guests. Many of the tour directors play this game called Moose Migration. In this game, each person is given a blank piece of paper and a crayon. The tour director then asks each person to draw a part of the moose. For example the director might say "Draw the body" then each person draws the body. Then they are to pass their papers forward one side and backward the other. "Draw the dulap. Pass papers, draw something to show the gender, pass papers, draw the face, etc."

What the game becomes is riotous laughter—because people draw breasts and penis onto their moose. It's actually great fun, but I've never chosen to play. I think I may be inwardly something of a prude, because I just don't feel the humor is sophisticated enough to justify the three grand most of these people have dealt out to be on the tour.

Another game that is played by many of the tour directors is Two Truths and a Lie. In this game you pass out index cards and the people are to write two things that have truthfully happened to them in their lives and one thing that did not happen to them.

We vote out loud on the one we feel is the lie. I played this game a couple of times last year and only once this year.

Most of the time this is fun and we find out hobbies and interests, which works well for people going to the ship, common interests can lead to friendships on their seven day cruise. But this year, there was a card that reminded me why I had stopped doing this game the year before. I think I remember the woman's name, Mrs. Vanderpelt. Anyway she had written:

1) I raced my husband's Porsche in a state race
2) My tomatoes won a ribbon at last year's county fair
3) My husband bought me a one carat diamond for this trip

When we all guessed the middle fact to be the lie she roared with laughter.

"Can you imagine *me* growing tomatoes?"

"No, Mrs. Vanderpelt. We couldn't."

————

Being an ex-elementary school teacher, I had no problems managing time so that the guests were always active in some way on tours #3 and #4. The problem stated, by many of this year's new tour directors, was the restaurant that was chosen to be our lunch stop: J. and J.

We must drive about five hours to get from Anchorage to Denali Park, so a lunch stop is imperative. Last year's lunch stop had been the Trapper Creek Lodge, which actually was more of a bar than a restaurant, so the tourists would consistently be confronted by drunk patrons, who wanted to argue. I found it to be entertaining, especially because the service was so slow that many of the guests got about half drunk themselves before their food would come.

We, the tour directors had been promised that J. and J. was much more of a restaurant in a rustic location. I hated that word rustic. In the tourism business, rustic means crummy.

So, as Mike, my motor coach driver approached J. and J. for our lunch, I rather nervously clutched my sandwich list in my hands.

The sandwich list was a requirement of J. and J. As I met the people, who flew into Alaska from locations most varied, at our Anchorage hotel, I had to ask them what kind of sandwich they preferred for lunch the next day. The choices were: two cold entrees; ham on white bread or roast beef on white bread and five hot entrees; hamburgers, cheeseburgers, buffalo burgers, musk ox burgers, or salmon patties. On the bottom of the sandwich list I got from my office was a rather disconcerting addendum, "Choice of either potato salad or cole slaw."

Now, the people were going to be paying $8.95 for their sandwich and to be only offered potato salad or cole slaw, somehow this smelled like trouble to me. My final tally was: 2 roast beef, 1 ham, 12 salmon patties, 6 buffalo burgers, 5 hamburgers, 6 cheeseburgers, and 2 musk ox burgers; brave souls there. I was supposed to fax this sandwich list to J. and J. at 9 AM. But, *not* after 10 AM the morning that we come. But, just to make sure, I faxed it to them the night before, which presented another problem.

J. and J. phoned my office to say that I hadn't faxed the list to them between 9 AM and 10 AM. My bosses in Anchorage radioed our motor coach and I had to relay my tally list to them on the radio, another reason I nervously clutched my list as our passengers disembarked.

"Remember, this is a very remote location," I had prepped my passengers as we had pulled up, "These people are trying their best."

We walked into a rather large dining hall with tables against the far wall. It actually looked clean. However, I saw no food on the long table that was set up.

"Are you with that tour group?" an older grey haired lady, who looked like she had just woke up and whose hair was going in angles it really shouldn't be able to said, "We're not ready for you yet."

I noticed my fax in her hands. "It's right at 12 noon," I countered. "Most groups are late."

"What are we supposed to do?" I asked trying to remain calm in this increasingly Rod Sterling type environment, "And isn't that my fax in your hands. My office said you didn't get it."

She then got right in my face and I could smell alcohol on her breath. "I guess I was wrong then, wasn't I? You should have faxed it in when you were supposed to! We'll bring the food out. Tell your 'old farts' to be patient." She then walked away.

Mike, my driver, came in. "What's going on?"

"You don't want to know," I said looking at the 32 faces searching for some semblance of food. Then, a young man with tattoos etched up both arms brought in a tray that had two roast beef and one ham sandwich, along with 14 small containers of potato salad and 20 small containers of slaw. As he dispensed the food onto the long table, I heard a few comments about the filthy REDRUM tee shirt he was wearing.

From nowhere, the evil, grey-haired lady reappeared. "This is where you announce that the cold sandwiches are ready. You're new here, aren't you?" she sneered.

I made the announcement and a few confused looking people made their way up to the table. "What will be next?" I asked desperately as she made an exit.

"Buffalo burgers, of course!" she didn't turn around.

When I turned back to the table, I noticed that all three sandwiches were gone. Someone, in their hunger, had taken my roast beef sandwich—more trouble.

"Hey Fred," It was Mike, the driver who looked rather ominous with his Wilfred Brimley mustache aboard the 78 inch frame— my guess as to why the psychotic proprietors were leaving him alone. He was motioning me to the swinging door that led into the kitchen. I looked in with him and saw the evil grey-haired lady taking a drag on a long cigarette, two younger guys, one with the REDRUM tee shirt, grabbing handfuls of raw hamburger with their bare hands—no plastic gloves here—and pressing them into flat patties to throw onto a thousand degree grill, and a truly psychotic looking short grey-haired man with a Hitler-like mustache lifting a platter I guessed had the six Buffalo burgers on it.

"I don't think that they are big into hygiene here at the J. and J." Mike quipped, "Health inspectors probably don't make it up this road."

"My guess is that the Bookmobile never gets up this way either."

"All the buffalo burgers are here!" Hitler announced as he neared the table. Evidently Eva Braun, his mate, had clued him into my lack of timing.

Only four people claimed their Buffalo burgers. So, it was a Buffalo-burger-bastard who had claimed my roast beef sandwich! I glanced around the room and noticed some impatient grimaces coming from the 23 people whom were yet to be served. I smiled and announced that the food was on its way.

When I took this job last year, it was with pride. I had researched our company and had found that this multi-billion dollar company, was looked upon by the cruise line industry as being their standard. Now 14 months later, I stood smiling at my guests realizing that they were about to eat from a facsimile of Larry, Daryl, and Daryl's Minutemen diner, from the old *Bob Newhart Show*.

I really had no choice. This was the only restaurant on this lonely road and the only thing worse than unhappy people at a restaurant would be hungry, unhappy people on a motor coach with me. I would get them through this experience somehow and hopefully the Denali Hotel we would be staying at this evening would have stomach pumps.

"The salmon and musk ox burgers are ready!"

Adolf had snuck behind me and I jumped at his announcement.

"Hey Fred," Mike whispered, "Did you order anything for me?"

I nodded and grabbed the two, somewhat warm, buffalo burgers and we headed for the lone empty table.

"Why did you choose a buffalo burger for us?" Mike asked as we sat and surveyed the two sandwiches, one container of slaw and another container of potato salad. The containers couldn't have held more than two tablespoons each.

"Obviously, you have never had the pleasure of tantalizing your taste buds with a buffalo entree before," I said and watched Mike slowly lift the top bun to reveal this blackened breaded patty that quite possibly was under-cooked.

"I'm so hungry, I could eat my grandmother's dingle berries," Mike continued and we both laughed. I liked this guy and was now glad that someone had taken my roast beef sandwich, otherwise Mike might have believed I was trying to poison him.

I noticed that the Nazi's leader had now brought in the hand-pressed hamburgers and cheeseburgers and had no need to make any announcement—the last of our group stood around the table like vultures waiting for anything to arrive.

I had forced about half of my buffalo burger down when Mr. Manning interrupted me. I remembered Mr. Manning's name because he was somewhat overweight and had larger boobs than any woman I had ever dated. So, in my mind he was the opposite of a man.

"I ordered a cheeseburger Fred, and he didn't bring enough out," Mr. Manning said and I noticed a twinkle in his eye. I couldn't help but think that maybe some of the other people also had noticed my mental analogy and he now knew I would have to confront our Fuhrer.

I walked to the table and saw that there was one lonely salmon patty sandwich unclaimed. I took a deep breath and approached my German nemesis, who stood looking somewhat satisfied as he surveyed all that was his.

"Excuse me, one of my customers didn't get a cheeseburger he had ordered," I tried not to sound intimidated. He slowly reached into his pocket and pulled out the now rumpled fax I had so stupidly sent the night before.

"This is what you ordered" he snickered, "We made what you ordered." His voice was calm and I swear I caught a bit of a German accent.

It was then that Eva came rushing out of the kitchen, blowing the last puff of her quick cigarette. "What's the problem now?" she yelled loud enough for a hush to come over my guests.

"There's no problem," I tried to remain calm, "You just need to cook another cheeseburger. One of my guests didn't get the one he ordered."

She ran and grabbed the now cold salmon patty sandwich and brought it back to show to her master. "Oh, I get it now." Adolf said and goose-stepped to where everyone was eating.

"May I have everyone's attention!" It immediately got quiet. I couldn't believe what I was witnessing.

"Someone in here ordered a salmon patty sandwich and took this man's cheeseburger. Who did it?" The last three words he said with such a reverberation that it frightened me.

I heard an older lady in the corner whimper, and everyone turned toward her. I stepped in before he could break her down.

"Why don't you put the salmon patty sandwich in the back under a heat lamp? You know our other motor coach should be arriving any second. It can be sold to one of them." I said this in a whisper, so that he might not view me as trying to usurp his authority and send me to the Western Front.

That seemed to bring him back to the twenty-first century and amazingly the kid with the REDRUM tee shirt brought out a cheeseburger. I didn't even want to consider its genesis, and handed it to Mr. Manning, who was laughing at the situation. His boobs were bouncing. I staggered back to the table. "That was fun," Mike dead panned. "And by the way, as long as you live on this planet, don't ever order me another buffalo burger."

The next 15 minutes seemed to go well and Mike and I made our way outside to wait for the customers to reboard the motor coach. "I think this place has changed ownership since I came in here with my motor-sickle buddies last Fall. It definitely wasn't this weird," It was then that our dictator stuck his head out the door.

"Fred, I need you in here, right now!"

Oh Lord, I thought, suddenly getting religion. I walked in to see Mr. Morganthal standing before the cash register, looking perplexed. "What's the problem?" I asked.

"He won't pay the tip!!" Hitler explained pointing to some small print that was on the menu—15% tip required in groups of more than six.

"This shouldn't apply. This is for sit down dinners," I appealed.

"It does, and I want my money."

"Do you want me to beat him up?" I laughed.

"I am calling your office and tell Jane about you—Fred! Hitler's face was red.

"Go for it Adolf," I said and most of my customers laughed.

I got my best tips of the season from that group and although, a

A view we got of Mount McKinley our guests got to see shortly after leaving J. and J.

few weeks later no other groups were allowed to stop at J. and J. I had found it quite entertaining—I love Alaska.

Let's Give Him a Hand

We've all done it—said things we wish we hadn't. Words that drift out of our mouths at the wrong time and the wrong place—almost as if the words didn't originate in our own heads.

Mackenzie had this happen to her during the second year of our company's existence. She was only 22 years old at the time and it turned out to be the last year she served as a tour director. Yet, when I reminded her of it, when I ran into her recently at the Fairbanks Airport, I could see her cringe. It was that full body cringe that impels me to make this story public.

Mackenzie and I were on a five day tour together that began in Fairbanks and ended in Anchorage with the guests then flying home. It had been a rather nondescript week with the guests only expressing minor disappointments about a rainy time of the summer.

I was standing in the main lobby of the Talkeetna Alaskan Lodge watching six of my guests listening to the K-2 Aviation representative telling them that the weather was marginal, and if they still wanted to fly to the lower glaciers around Mt. McKinley, they would give them a discount. None of my guests chose that option, so I was left to now consider dinner.

Mackenzie had no flyers, K-2 Aviation sign ups, and had headed back to her room earlier to change out of her uniform and thus be able to down a few beers in the bar at the hotel. So, it was to my surprise when she, still in her uniform, came running toward me. Her face was twisted in a strange smile and her usual red cheeks were now devoid of color.

Her duress involved one of her guests, Igor Mashinsky, whom we had been watching all week. Igor was in his late 60s and was a rather quiet man whose major distinguishing feature was that he was missing his right hand. Mackenzie had expressed early on that she couldn't stop herself from staring at the stump on the end of his right arm. There was a strangely designed mixture of scarred skin that resembled a swastika, thus my own perverse humor had driven a Nazi connection all week and I had managed a few laughs.

But, what precipitated Mackenzie's flight toward me was infinitely more enjoyable to my concept of levity.

Mackenzie felt some relief to be able to get to her room early, having none of her 36 guests sign up for any land excursions on this rainy evening, but as most things happen in her job as tour director, this feeling of relief was short lived. Between her and her room # 356, stood Igor Mashinsky and his traveling companion Peter. They were arguing about something to do with whether to take the shuttle down to the downtown area of Talkeetna for dinner. Mackenzie stepped in and began explaining to them the different options they had for evening activities. Both men seemed pleased that she was taking the time to help them out, but they both noticed that Mackenzie was staring at Igor's stump as she talked. Igor was used to this and smiled to himself as he pulled his stump up and slowly scratched behind his right ear. At that same time a lady exited from her room # 354, right beside them. The heavy oak stained door slammed shut with a rather loud boom. This loud interruption spawned a somewhat pregnant silence among the three people standing in the hall and somewhere within Mackenzie came the following words; "Boy, those heavy wooden doors sure could be dangerous. A person could lose a hand."

Igor looked down at his stump and then gave a rather stoic look to Mackenzie. Mackenzie's options were rather limited. She was totally mortified at what she had just said and in the few seconds that her mind outlined possible apologies, her young age gave her, her best option—she turned and ran.

Fouled Mouthed Kim

Tour #16 is a rehash of last year's tour #12, with a few changes, but is still loaded with many opportunities for self satire.

This is my third season as a tour director. In this type of seasonal work, it is necessary that you be invited back each year. The manager who makes this decision usually bases his or her decision upon whether you have had positive comment cards from the guests, you get along well with the vendors, and most importantly whether you can get along well with your fellow tour directors and motor coach drivers.

Since I view this job most of all as an opportunity to develop new routines, I make a supreme effort to satisfy the authorities.

I have noticed a pattern in my life that this particular position seems to neatly fit into. From 1965 until 1975 I worked summers as a sort of carney traveling to 20 or so County and State Fairs selling Pronto Pups (hot dogs on a stick) and lemonade shake ups. This experience seemed to lead me toward a life that wished to swim against the stream and finding a life in Alaska seemed to be the natural result. Then from 1984 until 1994, Celia and I invested in a computerized portrait business that traveled to forty or so communities in Alaska, Hawaii, and Illinois. This job, although more technical in nature, still involved seasonal work and thus humorous routines were an ongoing part of the script. Thus, based upon the ten year spans of my other seasonal jobs, I see that my tour directing career will probably run its course by 2011.

My pursuit of laughter in this life is more easily sated by seasonal jobs. My 26 years as a school teacher contained only one school year, 1981-1982, that I can honestly say had more laughter than frustration.

Back to tour #16. This story did not happen to me, but was told in detail to me by the tour director whom had the misfortune to experience it. This tour just happened last week. (I usually wait until the end of the season to allow the half dozen or so stories which have been developing in my head to synthesize.) The tour director's name is Kim. Kim is a mid-20s beauty who is in her first year as a tour director. I met Kim at one of our preseason meetings and the topic of whether she had a boyfriend came up as Garrett and I grilled the new employees.

"They give me a headache," was Kim's flippant reply, which serves as a foreshadowing for today's story.

I had seen Kim last Monday night at The Bluffs Hotel in Denali National Park. She ate dinner with Kristin, Nancy, and me and was expressing frustration over tour 16 already.

I had decided that I liked Kim because of two reasons. First of all, she would look at you directly in the eyes when she spoke to you and always spoke in an honest and gentle manner, and secondly she had no problem using the F word as a noun, adjective, verb, or adverb in her expressions. I have developed a prejudice of sorts in this regard. It just seems that people who are comfortable with themselves and their gift of the English language have no problem using profanity in ways that express an idea or piece of humor in more colorful ways. Certainly, there are extremes where profanity quickly becomes less appealing. My good friend Mark has a friend whom can use the F word as every part of speech in the same sentence. This quickly becomes tedious.

In the same regard, people who are overly uncomfortable using profanity or being around people who use profanity can be equally as tedious. I guess that this prejudice of mine equates to the fact that I don't have many friends.

It was the morning after I saw Kim that her adventure on tour 16 really began. Tour 16 mandates that the 35 guests Kim was hosting should awaken at 4 AM, put their bags in the hall, and get in line to be picked up at 5 AM by the Denali Tour bus. People in their late 60s and 70s, do not like to be pressed for time. I guess because they so little of it left. The TWT (Tundra Wilderness Tour) would last for eight hours and take them 55 miles into Denali National Park. During this time, the guests might see grizzly bears, Dall sheep, moose, wolves, caribou, ptarmigan, golden eagles, falcons, lynx, fox, and wolverines. But generally they would only see a few of the total species and those views were had only with high powered binoculars. It was this reality that possessed Kim's bus driver Jess* into the role he played daily for his sleep deprived passengers.

Jess is one of around a hundred drivers who spend their entire summer driving 400,000 tourists into the park on the single road that bisects an area the size of Massachusetts. The offshoot of this career choice is that somewhere around the end of June each summer most of the drivers lose their minds. Jess's glazed look went undetected by Kim as she entered the bus with her dazed guests.

Jess was around six foot four in height and had thinning blonde hair and he proudly announced that this was the tenth year that he had been a tour bus driver in Denali National Park. This yearly total was a symbol of pride amongst the tour drivers, because there were some who had been driving in the park for 25 years. Park driving was addictive for two reasons as I saw it. First, the money wasn't too bad, (Some drivers could average reasonable tips also.) and second, the sheer beauty of the landscape and surprise of what you would encounter on each drive into the park. Also, there existed a sort of camaraderie with all Denali Park employees that was renewed each May.

Jess' plan of attack upon the sensibilities of the aging ones was to stress his relationship to the land. He was married to an Athabascan Indian and so, he had mentally become native himself. He told native tales along the way, those stories that I have come to hate in my decade of experiences in village Alaska. The stories always are based upon the personalities of the native animals whom live along side Native Alaskans. New arrivals to Alaska are taken in by the simplicity of the native stories. But, from my 34 year perspective, they are incredibly boring. Okay. I know I should have more empathy. But, hearing about that old trickster raven and how he stole the sun and how the other animals ganged up on him to get their light back, makes me sigh just writing about it.

Anyway, Kim had no idea what Jess was up to when he pulled his bus off to the side of the road and asked everyone to sit and listen to the beauty of the silence. He then pulled a skin drum from behind his seat and asked everyone to get off the bus, that he had a surprise for them. This walk into the Native World always coincided with having a poor animal viewing day.

These people were at the total mercy of this madman and they knew it. Kim sighed a few profanities to herself and stepped onto the dusty road with everyone else.

Jess began beating his drum. Boom! Boom! Boom!

"You are entering *boom* a time thousands of years ago when only *boom* a few bands of Athabascan Indians frequented this beautiful *boom* park." Jess then pulled a huge wooden raven mask from his bus. Boom! Boom! Boom!

"That trickster, the raven *boom* had stolen the sun from the *boom* animals of the earth." Jess then had the group count off by fives and we had seven grizzlies, seven sheep, seven moose, seven wolves, and seven lynx. Boom! Boom! Boom!

He handed the huge heavy wooden raven mask to Kim and asked her to put it on. All other tour guides ever stuck with Jess before had declined the dreaded mask, but Kim didn't know any better and wanted to be a good sport. Boom! Boom! Boom!

As other tour buses passed by *boom* covering our dancing 70-year-old animals *boom* with road dust as they danced around the sweating Kim who was strapped into the 20 pound *boom* raven mask, something inexplicable happened. Kim was instructed to try and peck the other *boom* animals away, and when one of the bears, who also happened to be *boom!* a 70-something dirty old man whom had been copping feels from Kim all week, reached in for another *boom!* on a helpless, pecking raven with firm breasts. Kim tried to peck him hard but lost her footing and fell to the ground *boom!*

Kim screamed and the dancing old ones stopped and the native loving Norwegian Jess, whom, if he were truly following his heritage should be celebrating the fact that his Viking relatives raped and pillaged natives from Greenland to Eastern Canada and back, set down his drum. Kim pulled off the torturous mask and felt a bump rising on her forehead.

The man who caused her fall reached down to help her but she was still in a daze. Get away from me you frigging bear!" Kim yelled, then felt embarrassed as she realized the situation.

The rest of Kim's tour #16 was filled with ice packs and sympathetic guests. She did well with tips and wrote up Jess for his acid-trip—like raven mask, bus choreography.

Jeem

Tour #19 is the same as Tour #13 from the previous two years. You meet the guests in Fairbanks on Saturday night, spend two nights there, train to Denali Park for one night, train to Talkeetna for two nights, then spend the final night together at the Alyeska Resort in Girdwood, before motor coaching to the ship on the final day. Tour directors generally love this tour because it is the longest of the 19 tours, which equates to more hours logged, thus a higher salary, and if you happen to mix well with your guests, you'll also accrue more tips.

I saw this tour as a double-edged sword in that yes, you could make more lucre, but, should you end up with conglomeration of guests whom, for whatever reason, tried your patience, you will need to discover burgeoning mental blueprints to prevent your hands from encircling the neck of the woman from New Jersey who wants "a monetary refund' because Mount McKinley is hiding behind the clouds."

This tour, of which I am about to share, concerns a different tour director. His name is Jim and he is from around the Pittsburgh area of Pennsylvania. Jim has also been with our company since the company began in 2001. He is around a dozen years younger than me and I have always enjoyed touring with him. With Jim, what you see is what you get. He is honest and not afraid to tell anyone who tests his resolve, exactly what he thinks about them. I enjoy witnessing those moments when Jim's patience is tested. There is a vein in the left side of Jim's neck that swells up as he explains to all those around him that they have entered into Jim's world and they should back off. He was a manager of a large trucking outfit in the Pittsburgh area for years. Jim was a motor coach driver his first year and switched to being a tour director his second year.

Jim was in the office when I stopped in on a Thursday, after dropping a group of guests off in downtown Anchorage for lunch. He was going over his manifest for his upcoming tour #19.

"How many have you got?" I asked as I scanned the tour directors room for any semblance of sugary treats.

"Forty-four, no kids, no wheelchairs; but, there is a couple from Brazil who speak only broken English." Jim responded.

"You know what I smell?" I smiled. "Empty envelopes?"

Jim sneered up at me, "Once they hear *The Jim Story* they will fill the envelope with pesos."

"Jim, they won't understand a word you say and Brazil is Portuguese in origin, so no pesos." I responded and realized that no food items existed here and the word pesos had set off a response mechanism that had taken control.

"I'm walking to the Mexican food stand, want me to bring you a burrito?" I asked.

"No, I'm meeting Nancy for lunch. Hey, I think you are on a #19 and I am on a #20 in two weeks. I'll let you know then how I wowed the Brazilian contingent when we meet up at Sophie's Hotel."

I left and when I returned 20 minutes later with my Burrito Deluxe, I also got one for Jane and Mark, so, I wouldn't be the only one dribbling taco sauce off my chin, Jim had departed.

It was two weeks later that the details of his tour #19 were brought forward.

Jim related to me that this tour #19 had been fairly normal until they got to Talkeetna on the fourth day. Oh, there had been the usual irritations that come with all tours. A couple was angry that Sophie's Station, our hotel in Fairbanks for this tour, did not offer a shuttle to take them to The Pump House restaurant for dinner.

To all of our hotel's credit, they want the guests to stay and eat

Jeeem, as he was explaining this story to me.

at their restaurants. Jim had to raise his voice briefly during this crisis. Also, in Denali National Park, Jim had the misfortune of getting Jess, the raven hat driver. But Jim already knew of Kim's misadventure's with this psycho driver earlier in the season, so he told a shaken Jess that there would be no animal dancing on this tour. A trait of Jim's that went along with his bulging neck vein was that, almost like an octopus, Jim's facial color could become a bright red at the moment someone irritated him.

When they got to Talkeetna, Jim felt, as most tour directors do, that it would be all down hill from here. This tour has a day on their own in Talkeetna, so aside from seeing off land excursions people had signed up for, it was a day to relax. Unfortunately for Jim, it would be all uphill from here.

Jim had just settled into his room, after having a steak dinner with Jennifer, Stephen, and Stephanie. The three other tour directors were about half his age, but were fun to talk with. All four tour directors had announced their intentions, with only three weeks left in the season, that this would be their final year of tour directing.* Stephen and Stephanie had just announced their engagement, and Jim was secure in the fact that he would have the room to himself until Stephen would straggle in during the wee hours of the morning.

*In the three summers that I have tour directed I found that toward the end of each season most tour directors talk of not returning the next season, but when we all meet the following May, I see many of those same complainers back again. I call their returning the Spin and Marty Syndrome, which was an old TV show that was attached to The Mickey Mouse Club. In it, young boys would meet each summer at a six week summer camp on which their parents sent them. I remember how excited they were to see each other again. Few tour directors see each other in the off season, so this excitement exists for them also.

The phone rang and Jim sighed. "Hello, this is Jim," Jim responded in his tour director voice.

"Meeester Jeeem? this is Mrs. Mendez I require talk with you."

Jim didn't give me their names so the only Brazilian I know of is Sergio Mendez and Brazil 66 'an old music group. "What is this about?" Jim talked slow knowing that his Brazilian couple knew little English, but had been no problem so far and had seemed to truly enjoy the beauty of Alaska.

"Meeester Jeeem", she hesitated and sounded panicked.

" I'll be in the lobby in five minutes." Jim said.

"Oh, thank you Meeester Jeeem!" Mrs. Mendez responded.

What's this going to be all about? Jim thought,' and started putting his uniform back on.

Around five minutes later Jim walked into the lobby of the Talkeetna Alaskan Lodge and saw Mrs. Mendez standing in front of the 40-foot river rock fireplace. She was a short woman, probably in her mid-forties, but with her long black hair hanging over her shoulders, and with the stressful look that had taken possession of her face, she looked 20 years older.

"Oh, thank you Meeester Jeeem," she ran up to him and put her arms around him.

Jim looked around, feeling somewhat embarrassed.

"What is the problem, Mrs. Mendez?" Jim asked and pushed back from the woman.

"It's Sergio, heee's hoooiting"

"What?"

"Hoooiting," Jim gave her a confused look.

Mrs. Mendez was searching for a word he might understand.

"Heee's got pain." she finally managed.

"Oh," Jim responded "He's hurting"

"Yes, hoooiting"

"Where is he hurting?" Jim responded as the German-imported night desk girl Claudia walked past them and winked at Jim.

Mrs. Mendez's face turned red as she moved both of her hands down between her legs.

"Down there," she managed, "It's one of hees round theengs".

"One of hee's round theengs? ... his balls?" Jim asked.

"Yes Jeeem, hee's balls," Mrs. Mendez was excited and Jim wanted to hide, "theees one ball" she pointed to the right side of the inside of her legs, "is getting beeeegger"

She looked like she might cry, "Meeester Jeeem it's sooo beeeg!"

Jim had Mrs. Mendez sit next to the fireplace and went to the check in counter. He talked with Claudia for a bit and then went to use the phone that was on the wall next to the counter. A few minutes later he walked over and approached Mrs. Mendez.

"Mrs. Mendez, I phoned the clinic here in Talkeetna and they said that we can bring your husband." Jim looked at his watch and spotted the next piece of his puzzle walking out of the restaurant.

"Excuse me, Mrs. Mendez," Jim said and walked to intercept Heather, one of our company representatives, who was stationed in Talkeetna.

'This conversation might be fun,' Jim thought to himself as he approached the cute, 26-year-old blonde from New Hampshire who had found this job on the internet and had come here for adventure. Heather had been having dinner with some of the younger male drivers and was now going to get the company van to take them out to the Paradise Lodge, where all the motor coach drivers stayed while in Talkeetna.

"Heather we have a problem," Jim said as he approached the perky blonde.

"Oh yeah, what's up?" She responded flashing her million dollar smile.

"It really isn't about what is up. It more concerns what is getting bigger." Jim said and Heather gave him a curious look.

"Now promise me you won't laugh, my guest is sitting at the fireplace watching us."

Heather agreed, becoming immensely more curious.

"Mr. Mendez, a Brazilian guest of mine, has a testicle, his right one I believe, that is swelling uncontrollably."

" What is making it swell?" Heather asked, giving Jim a wry smile thinking he was putting her on.

"Do you see Mrs. Mendez sitting there? If you want to go ask her what she did to make his right testicle get bigger, go for it, but she says he is really hoooiting and we need to get him to the clinic."

"He's what?"

"Hurting, silly," Jim giggled, "We need to get him to the clinic. Can you pull up in front here with the van in ten minutes?"

"I need to take the drivers out to Paradise."

"Go tell them to order some more fries. This won't take you an hour, I'm guessing." Jim then walked back to Mrs. Mendez.

Thirty minutes later Jim was back in his room shaking his head over the strangeness of the past hour.

The next morning, Jim had to drag himself to the lobby to see three of his guests off on a 5 AM fishing excursion. He always tried to steer the fishing idiots to go on the 4 PM fishing excursion, but these were Nebraska people who bragged "that 5 AM was late breakfast for them." There were no phone messages or messages waiting for him at the front desk so he assumed that the caper of the previous evening had come to a positive conclusion.

He returned to the lobby at 9 AM to see off some guests who were going flightseeing with K-2 Aviation to see Mt. McKinley. It was a beautiful day and the six guests were excited as the white K-2 van arrived and whisked them off.

It was late enough in the morning and Jim remembered my words about empty envelopes and the Brazilians, so he decided to phone their room and do a follow up.

"Good morning Mrs. Mendez. How is your husband doing?"

"Ohhhh, Jeeem. Please come to our room. It's three, five, one." She then hung up.

Jim sighed and walked to the East Wing. *They have a view room. They probably just want to show off the view to me*, Jim thought as he knocked on their door.

Mrs. Mendez opened the door and pulled Jim by the arm into their room. Jim suddenly was standing at the end of Sergio's bed looking at a man who was lying there nude, except for the white sheet pulled up just below his waist. What alarmed Jim almost more than this incredibly bizarre situation was the amount of chest hair Sergio had. The hair was so thick, that it looked as if it were parted in three or four places.

This guy's wolf man, no wonder things are happening. It's probably a full moon. Jim thought to himself, trying to hold back a giggle.

There was such a grimace on Sergio's face it was hard to look

at him. But the bulge in the sheet where his penis was, was difficult not to stare at. Jim remembered the old elephantiasis movies
from high school.

"Jeeem. It really hoooits. Pleeeze do something. Do you want
me show it to you?" Sergio managed.

"No!" Jim said and was sure that the vein on his neck was pro-
truding, "I'm no doctor."

"Is it going to boooist?" Mrs. Mendez asked as Jim was weigh-
ing in any possible way he could quickly escape this room. He
spotted a bottle of medicine sitting by the bed that obviously had
had no effect.

"What?" Jim asked.

"Boooist," then Mrs. Mendez made her hands small and then
flicked them open quickly.

"Oh burst. Oh, I hope not. I'll get an ambulance here." Jim said
and fled the room.

Jim called the hospital in Palmer and an ambulance was sent
and was expected to arrive around noon. He then called the Mendez room to inform them and had a bellman take a bottle of aspi-
rin to help with the pain. Jim never wanted to re-enter that room.

Around noon the ambulance arrived and while the EMTs were
in the process of wheeling Sergio out, a helicopter swooped down
and hovered over the hotel entrance. It so happened, that a guest
on the northbound morning train had suffered a heart attack and
had already been airlifted by this helicopter, but somehow, word
of Sergio's dilemma had gotten around Talkeetna, and the helicopter pilot thought he was also supposed to pick him up.

"Where is the man with the swollen testicle?" a loud speaker attached to the bottom of the helicopter asked. Amanda, the hotel
manager waved her arms, trying to express to the helicopter that
they weren't needed.

Jim spotted Heather in the crowd and saw that she had her

short wave radio in hand. Being a manager of a trucking concern, Jim knew the emergency frequency on that radio and radioed to the helicopter that their services were not needed.

The helicopter and the ambulance left around the same time and Jim was able to take his deepest sigh of the season.

Surgery had to be done on Sergio and he rejoined the group in Girdwood. He tipped Jim what he should have, but gave Jim average marks on the evaluation sheet.

My guess is that Jim would have gotten higher marks had he looked under the sheet.

Mrs. Brown

I was in the lobby of the Grande Denali Hotel making sure that my 49 guests had found their rooms and were satisfied. We had just arrived at Denali National Park on the 4 PM northbound train. Tour 14 begins at the Marriott Hotel in Anchorage and works its way to Fairbanks with two days of train legs, breakfast and lunch. Once the Fairbanks' day is over on Friday, the tour groups jet back to Anchorage and motor coach down to their cruise ship in Seward.

This tour was tour 11 last year and usually presented problems in the logistics of putting the right groups of people onto the two Alaska Airlines jets that were assigned for this purpose. Guests who were traveling with other couples and were separated in any manner during their trip had a tendency to flip out. The flight south was only 39 minutes, but represented a breach in the expectations of the guests who had become mentally secure with the notion that they would be umbilically attached to their friends during the five day duration of this land tour.

I was preparing myself for this psychological possibility and also sighing a bit because I was also entertaining my older sister *Cheryl and her husband Rich on this tour. I had contacted my office in April to make sure that I would be their tour director and now the trip Cheryl had planned 13 months earlier was becoming reality.

Unfortunately, up to this point, I hadn't had much free time to spend with them. I was up late each night writing vouchers for all of the land excursions people were signing up for.

   * I had some trepidation about being my older sister's tour director because of a few things that had happened in our childhood. The first experience of recall might seem trivial, but I believe that it set up a model for me in later life. Our mother would buy Fig Newton cookies once a week and I loved, and still love, them—anyway Cheryl would watch me like a hawk and make hourly reports to Mom or Dad as to how many Newtons I had consumed.

   Sometimes I would act like I was walking from the living room to the bathroom and then veer off to the back entrance to the kitchen, slowly opening the third drawer which held my sugary bounty, and ever so stealthily lift a single soft-filled cookie from the cellophane wrapper. Taking more than that single prize would involve more cellophane, causing a crinkling noise and chancing detection.

   Usually an attack on the Newton's on a Sunday evening when either the *Ed Sullivan Show* or the *Perry Mason Show* were on was a no brainer. The television in the Colvin household was always on, but these two favorite shows brought near hypnotic attention. A tornado might hit 8 Arizona Drive and we would still be lying on our couches trying to watch Topo Geego on the *Ed Sullivan Show*. Yet somehow Cheryl always knew the exact number of cookies I had taken. I think she was good at math. She did major in math her freshman year at Illinois State University.

The second incident involved a time when Cheryl and I were left alone to watch David and Judy. I really don't remember the genesis of Cheryl and my argument, but I believe that it involved me stealing Cheryl's autographed photo of Ed 'Kookie' Burns (who starred on the TV show *77 Sunset Strip*.—anyway, Cheryl was chasing me down the hallway trying to get Kookie's image from my grip and she slipped and slid into one of the main chairs to the new dining room set our parents had recently purchased. She shattered one of the legs of the poor, unknowing, and totally innocent chair. Cheryl and I both looked at each other in horror.

I ended up taking the blame for this adolescent indiscretion. To this day Cheryl believes that I actually did do the deed. This act, on my part, of taking the blame, so courageous and bold in nature, went completely unappreciated.

So, as I sighed in the lobby of the Grande Denali Hotel, I was approached by a desperate looking Mr. Brown.

"Fred, my wife is very upset!" the look in his eyes reflected a lifetime of fear.

There had been a mix up in the two families named Brown. One family had requested that their children's room be near them and the hotel had inadvertently placed the other couple with the Brown moniker next to them also. I hadn't foreseen this as a problem because the new room for the Brown couple was only three doors down from the other four couples they were traveling with. But, I had misjudged Mrs. Brown.

"Mr. Brown, the hotel is completely booked for this evening—there's really nothing we can do." I responded.

Mr. Brown looked down—as if his spirit had been sucked from this dimension. "Maybe, we can do something for tomorrow night," I further offered.

Mr. Brown stumbled away and I noticed that my sister had witnessed Mr. Brown's unhappiness and gave me a look like *if I wanted her assistance, she would be happy to step in for me.* I wondered if Mr. Brown had any Fig Newtons hidden somewhere in his room?

It wasn't five minutes later that Mrs. Brown came directly up to me—her husband trailing behind on an invisible leash that was psychologically noticeable.

I was expecting a loud voice of defiance—instead, out came this whining sound that revealed the prescript of Mrs. Brown, that all of her life she had been given everything she had wanted by whining and acting like a child. This was a milk toast plain, short, brown-haired woman in her early 50s, so this tact took me by surprise.

"I want to talk with the president of your company," she whined.

I hesitated—trying to assess the degree of her psychosis.

"We have been planning this vacation for years and have paid thousands of dollars," she started, when she was satisfied that I was not responding quick enough. "Your company has screwed us two other times!"

"I think that I can get you a room next to your friends for tomorrow night," I offered this bone while many of the other tour 14 guests watched the development of this mini-drama. Mrs. Brown then sniffed her nose, whimpered, and stepped close to me.

"I want to talk with your boss right now!" she said in a new guttural, earthy voice that, quite frankly, frightened me. I then started to feel some empathy for the leashed husband—for I now detected a look in her eyes that defied earthly definitions.

"I'll phone my boss in Anchorage," I whispered into the whimpering psycho's ear, "She is the boss over everyone who works in

Alaska." I then shook my head for effect to make her realize how important my boss was. (I have taught nine-year-olds for two decades and Mrs. Brown was mimicking their maturity.)

I phoned my boss, who listened attentively as I explained to her about Mrs. Brown and how the end of Western Civilization as we know it may come to an end unless she is transferred three doors closer to her friends.

She listened to Mrs. Brown for at least 10 minutes and the room full of guests watched in delight as Mrs. Brown broke down in tears on two occasions during the conversation.

I took the phone back and my boss and I agreed to give the Brown's two free breakfasts to alleviate some of the monumental stress created by this situation.

It was what happened after the phone conversation that I will always remember.

I told Mr. Brown of the two free breakfasts and he tiptoed to his distraught wife to tell her of the resolution's reward.

She didn't smile and then announced loudly to him. "I knew when I married a man with a common name like Brown, that someday something like this would happen!"

Mr. Brown whimpered.

I smiled.

Jack's Tour

This tour happened several years ago and doesn't even involve the company for whom I work. It was relayed to me in the most brief of descriptions, but I feel impelled to relay the heart of the story to you and will take liberties with the outlying facts as are necessary.

When I said other company, I should probably relay a few facts about the tourism business here in Alaska. The main four companies who bring tourists to Alaska are Princess, Holland America, Royal Caribbean/Royal Celebrity, and Carnival. Crystal Ships and some European Lines also bring ships here each summer, but their numbers don't match the big four. There are touring companies such as Premier who book land tours only for guests on the different ships and meet the ships when they arrive in Seward. Of the 750,000 guests who cruised to Alaska last summer, only about 20% made the trip across the Gulf of Alaska to Seward and entered my world. The majority of cruisers take the seven day tour from Vancouver, B. C. to Skagway and back. Virtually every room in all 16 ships we meet each summer is filled.

I have come upon a few thoughts on what motivates people to spend the extra money and cruise to Alaska. The Alaskan run is the most profitable for all of the cruise companies. It is much cheaper to cruise in the Caribbean.

Foremost, the majesty of Alaska's scenery grabs the imagination of so many, especially the east coasters, who spend much of their lives viewing the urban scenery. Secondly, the specter that they are traveling almost to a different country intrigues them. We get comments like 'Do you accept U.S. currency up here?' at least once a summer. There exists also a certain mystique or romance associated with a vacation to Alaska. Each summer I have several women and men who are traveling alone with another couple who tell me that all of their married life their spouse and they had planned a trip to Alaska, and although their spouse has passed away they are coming anyway.

The guest's motivations make me consider why Celia and I have chosen to spend the last 34 years of our lives up above sixty degrees north latitude. Today is November ninth. It is windy and 20 degrees outside. It is almost 9 AM and the sun hasn't really made an impression upon the day. These are simply realities that go along with the three dark months in the north. The first of November until the first of February are the times that try Alaskan's souls, no matter how long they have lived up here. I won't make up psychological excuses explaining how living through these times makes Alaskans any tougher than anyone else, because I don't believe that it is true. What we are is not a factor of where we are, it is more a factor of what we choose to do with the consciousness we are given. I believe that Celia and I have both followed the intuitive sides of our natures, and have inexorably chosen Alaska as the *proper and best* place to live and bring up our family. It will surprise me if any of our three children return to Alaska to live, for just as Celia and I fled central Illinois to pursue our own intuitive destinies, they should seek signs that will lead them on their own particular journeys.

I guess that since I named this story *Jack's Tour*, I should get back to that direction.

Jack is a new tour guide with our company this year. He is from Canada and had worked as a tour director previously for a competing company. He is a tall, thin man with jet black hair and probably in his late 20s. He *shadowed* with me the first week out and I got to know him. What impressed me was how accommodating and polite he was with guests. People come on these tours with a certain amount of angst, since most of them have never done anything like this before, I believe that an important function of what we do is to make our guests as comfortable as possible, as quickly as possible. Jack has that ability. I knew that his success with our company was assured the first time I saw him speaking with a guest. He also laughed at my jokes, which is a necessity in *Fred's World*.

I guess that I should explain a bit about why most of the previous tour stories I have attempted to be humorous. I have never tried to write comedy before and thought that this tour directing job could serve as a good basic structure to develop that skill. I have always thought there is a certain psychological strength to laughter. Throughout my life, I have attempted to find people to be around who weren't afraid to laugh and have made every effort to avoid being in too close of a proximity to serious minded people. Making people laugh and surrounding yourself with people who make you laugh is a prescription that can't be filled at a pharmacy, but laughter is a drug that will keep you alive and healthy. A recent study found that very young children laugh on average 400 times each day. Adults by comparison laugh only 40 times each 24 hours. As we age we evidently find our lives to be less comical or maybe closer to the truth, we choose to not look for the humor that *does exist* in most every moment.

I hope that people reading these stories do not feel that my intention is to belittle the actors who play the parts of my guests, during our summer melodramas. I simple wish to report the *hu-*

man condition, which I have always felt to be ultimately humorous. Events in all of our lives, if looked upon with a mature perspective, almost has to bring a grin to your face.

The thing that gets in the way in our little tourism world, as probably in most other worlds, are people's expectations. They expect events and weather to go a certain way on their Alaska adventure. These expectations are a major force in building the frown lines on their faces.

Mrs. Brown expected a room next to her friends, the ex-nun expected not to be seasick, Adolph, at J. and J. did not expect the belligerent group I took to him, and Jeeem, the tour director, did not expect to be viewing a hairy Brazilian man. These events are humorous and if you can't see the humor in them, I suggest you are laughing even fewer than 40 times each day. I would like to be a beneficiary on your life insurance policy.

Jack talking with guests.

Returning to Jack's tour.

Jack met his group of 44 guests in Skagway. As they disembarked from their cruise ship about two-thirds of them chose to take the White Pass Railroad trip to the top of White Pass. This was an excursion choice, so Jack had to shop around in Skagway with the dozen or so who chose not go railroading for an hour. Their motor coach would then drive up to the pass on one of the most scenic highways in the world, pick up the majority of their group, and continue to Whitehorse, Yukon to spend the night.

Six of his new group decided to hang out with Jack as they meandered around the crowded street of Skagway. Three other cruise ships were also in port. Skagway had more than 300 dockings that summer. The Patterson's seemed like a pleasant couple. Sheila was in a wheel chair and her husband Todd laughed with her as he pushed her along the boardwalks of Skagway's historic Main Street. They were in their mid-70s according to the manifest and Jack had some trepidation before he met them that he would need to provide extra service for them. But, this obviously was not going to be the case.

Jack walked slowly along with them and saw the Patrick's and the Whitmore's about a block ahead of them. The two couples ahead were traveling together and had complained that the $90 charge to take the White Pass Railroad was excessive. This was typical. The company Jack worked for at this time seemed to draw people at least ten years older, on average, than our company did.

"Jack," Mrs. Patterson interrupted Jack's thinking of how bored some of the young workers in the gift shops looked. "Look back at that glacier that seems to be hanging over the fjord. Isn't it breathtaking?"

"Yes," Jack responded, "Where are you from Mrs. Patterson?

"A little town in southern Illinois. Salem. Ever heard of it? I am 78 years old and this is the first time I have seen mountains in person."

"Hasn't your husband taken you anyplace?" Jack joked.

"We're farmers, Jack. We raised seven wonderful children and just never found much time to travel. Oh, we've been to St. Louis, Chicago, and even to Nashville once. But, nothing like this!" Mrs. Patterson just seemed to beam and her enthusiasm made Jack want to hang out with her husband and her.

They traveled the short distance of Skagway's main street, had a few snacks at a pizza shop, then headed back toward the dock where the motor coach would be waiting to take them. The dozen or so others were already in the bus as the Patterson's and Jack approached. The driver, an older, very gregarious guy named Cliff, let down the lift, which aided in boarding Mrs. Patterson and her wheelchair. This company had the driver in charge of narration, while Jack was simply meant to *mix* with the people and organize any land excursions they had booked separately. In many ways Jack preferred this system to the system of the tour director doing narration and organizing, but if you had the misfortune to get a driver who was not knowledgeable, a good people person, or simply hated you, then your tour could be seriously compromised.

The drive up the pass was beautiful as usual. Jack wondered if the people who lived in Skagway or Whitehorse took this incredible scenery for granted? The driver stopped at several pullouts so people could get photos looking across the valley at the train tracks, down the mountain to look back at Skagway and the brilliantly

Photo of Skagway that Mrs. Patterson bought in a gift shop and shared with Jack.

blue water of the Lynne Canal, and at the top of the pass at the mounds of snow, still not melted even though it was now mid summer.

As if on cue, they pulled into the area where the train turns around right as the White Pass engine was blowing it's whistle and pulling into the make shift station. Most of the passengers aboard the train would stay onboard and return to their cruise ship, but Jack would receive his 30 guests as would the other eight motor coaches waiting.

The trip up to Whitehorse took only a couple of hours and Jack busied himself getting everyone's flight-out information, once they reached Anchorage in eight days. He also presented the land excursion sheet to each couple so they could decide quickly what activities in Whitehorse, Dawson City, or Alaska they might want in addition to what was included in their tour plan.

There was a dinner theater that night in Whitehorse that was included in their tour, but Jack decided to stay at the hotel, having endured the off pitched singing of one *Miss Klondike Lil* half a dozen times already and he knew that his driver Cliff was a good guy and wouldn't nark on him to the front office.

Jack had purchased some fruit and snacks at the Fairway Market in Skagway, so he ate them instead of paying for an inflated priced dinner downstairs. Also, there was a hockey game on the TV. Being a Canadian, having no interruptions from guests, and getting to watch some quality professional hockey, put Jack as close to heaven as this job gets.

After the hockey game ended, a satisfied Jack went to the lounge to have a drink and maybe strike up a conversation about the game, which ended with the Edmonton Oilers winning 2-1.

The hotel was an older version, as was most of the hotels that this company chose to stay, and the very smoky lounge was filled with mid-aged men who were still worked up about the hockey game. Jack was immediately glad that he chose the quietude of his room to enjoy the game. He then spotted Mr. and Mrs. Patterson in the corner. He thought sure that he had checked all of the guests off as going to the dinner theater, which still had about 90 minutes until Cliff would be bringing them back.

Mr. Patterson was waving to Jack to come to their table.

Jack approached them amiably. "I thought you two were going to see Klondike Lil?"

"We decided to stick around here. Why don't you join us for a drink?" Mr. Patterson offered and Mrs. Patterson reached up with both of her hands and squeezed Jack's right hand.

Sheila Patterson's warm hands sped memories of Jack's grandmothers through his head. There was no way he wasn't going to join this sweet, gentle lady.

"Okay, thanks." Jack hesitated. It was always awkward trying to decide if it is appropriate to join the guests. If many of your guests are in a room, you don't want to imply favoritism.

"What'll ya' have mate?" the cute, perky blonde waitress with the Australian accent was right there to wait on him, and the real reason Jack always had a drink at this hotel.

Jack gave her a look.

"Oh, I remember. You're the Molson guy," she winked and returned to the bar, as every set of male eyes in the room recorded her strut on their testosterone-driven mental VCR's.

"She's a flirt," Todd Patterson commented with a smile, "A very attractive flirt."

"Calm down, old man!" Sheila Patterson punched her husband in the arm. "Jack, you must have a girlfriend somewhere, you're such a good looking young man."

"No, I haven't had too much luck with the women," Jack lamented.

"Oh, you will. I can see it in your hands. I've always been something of a fortune teller, haven't I Todd?" Her husband nodded and took another drink of what looked like a rum and coke. "I'm one eighth Choctaw and I think I've always favored my Indian side."

"One Molson for the tour director extraordinaire," the waitress returned with Jack's beer and leaned down touching him with her shoulder as she set the beer in front of him.

"Thanks," Jack offered, feeling his face getting a bit red.

"Todd, could you run back to the room and get that envelope I made out for Jack earlier this evening?" Sheila said, with her face taking on a more serious tone.

Todd didn't respond, but got up and slowly left the table.

"Todd gets upset when I bring this up," Sheila Patterson said and leaned closer to Jack, who had just finished his first healthy swig of beer, "But, I need to tell you something very important."

Jack set his beer down and looked curiously at the sweet, kindly, and now mysterious lady.

"I am not going to be able to finish this tour. I am really sorry and I wanted to let you know ahead of time, so it won't be too much of a shock."

"Are you and your husband meeting someone?" Jack asked looking confused.

Mrs. Patterson laughed, "I am, but not my husband. Jack, I am going to die. I know it will be very soon, Maybe tonight, maybe tomorrow. But I'm sure not any longer than that. Some people can tell when they will leave this life. I happen to be one of those people. The doctors gave me one month to live, six months ago, but Todd and I have been planning this trip for years and I wasn't going to let him down." She then looked whimsical, "this place is more beautiful than we could ever have imagined."

"I don't like to talk about this in front of Todd, so I won't after he comes back with the envelope. In the envelope there is a letter of apology I'd like you to read to the other guests on this trip and of course your tip money."

Todd Patterson then returned with the envelope and Sheila Patterson squeezed Jack's hand and leaned away from him. "Give the envelope to Jack, Todd. I've told him about the possibilities."

Todd nodded.

The next two hours seemed to flow past Jack and the three Molsons he consumed listening to the Patterson's. They talked about their life together and gave Jack little vignettes about each of their wonderful children. Jack was the necessary audience they needed for this evening.

Jack felt as if he were under a trance. The morbidity of Mrs. Patterson's admission seemed to transfix his attention away from the smoke-filled environment they shared and toward the infinite, which was the love that these two people had for one another.

Jack slept under this trance.

The next day when their motor coach was halfway to Dawson City and a tearful Mr. Patterson had Jack and Cliff stop the bus because his wife had passed away, it was a calm Jack who spoke to rest of the contingent and explained to them that they had no recourse but to prop Mrs. Patterson against the window in her seat and continue the final two hours to their destination as a very crowded hearse rather than a sightseeing bus.

It wasn't until seven days later and Jack had seen all of his guests off at Anchorage International Airport that the trance seemed to be wearing off. He would be meeting a new group of guests at the Westmark Hotel the next day and traveling back to Skagway going the opposite direction. Thus, he needed to do his laundry.

As he prepared a pair of pants, a white envelope fell from one of the pockets. It was as if someone had slapped Jack from reality. He opened the envelope and found a very generous tip and the sheet of paper Mrs. Patterson had written on to apologize for the inconvenience she might have caused. Jack couldn't read it. He could only glance at it. He saw a beautifully written document that almost looked like calligraphy. He noticed words like splendid and overpowering as she described the scenery she had seen.

The famous thinker Gurjieff stated that 99% of humanity lived their entire lives in a state of sleep. Reacting to outside stimuli, never really considering who or what they actually are. His famous quote was 'Until a man uncovers himself, he cannot see.'

As Jack sat on the edge of the bed in a very ordinary hotel room in Anchorage, Alaska, his head in his hands, and tears rolling down his cheeks, he had uncovered, with Mrs. Patterson's help, something about himself, and he knew that he was a better person because of it.

We're All Adults Here

It isn't easy being a guy. Women don't understand this. We are creatures of a raging conflict between hormones and morals.

The following is a short story that supports this premise.

It was summer solstice in Fairbanks, Alaska. Every hotel room in town was filled. Celebrating the longest day of sunlight at 64 degrees north latitude is a big deal, evidently. Personally, I don't get it. Okay, the sun is out for more than 22 hours; and barely dips below the horizon for an hour and a half. Does the sun know anything about this? And if it did, would it care? I doubt it.

Anyway, Pike's Waterfront Lodge found itself overbooked. And so, as all our hotels do when this happens, they kicked out the five tour directors who were scheduled to stay there with their groups. This left Brad, Bryan, J, Craig, and Joanna homeless for the night. Nancy, our Fairbanks director, an insanely pro Ohio State alumni, found an obscure Bed & Breakfast, and dispatched her five minions to the remote lodging in a company van.

The 20 mile road was dusty and the B&B turned out to be simply some guy's house. The five warily approached the aging residence as the van sped away. A lanky, dusty, gray-bearded man approached. "Ya know, I don't do this for everyone!" he screamed, and then spit at the swarm of mosquitoes now enveloping him.

"But Nancy's a Buckeye just like I am." He then walked them into the home, housing large dust bunnies, that danced like tumbleweed across an unswept hardwood floor.

"There's two beds downstairs, and one up. You kids divvy them up however you want. But, you have to be out by noon. Gotta have time to clean you know.

With that, the supposed innkeeper disappeared. In unison the five exhausted tour directors sighed. It was quickly decided that the beautiful, young Joanna should have the lone queen-sized bed upstairs. The two downstairs beds were singles. The four guys were left to discuss these marginally adequate accommodations.

Craig, the oldest at 33, knew that two of the younger guys were homophobic. A sort of pecking order for the other beds asserted itself.

Into the gentlemanly debate over sleeping arrangements, the lovely Joanna descended, more or less unexplained, wearing only sweatpants and a form fitting Victoria's Secret tee shirt. The four guys stared—pleased, but awkwardly aghast.

"Listen, guys," She announced, addressing the conundrum of beds, men, and women in as logical a manner as she could muster, "We're all adults here, and if one of you would like to come upstairs and sleep with me, it really isn't that big of a deal."

Now, this is the moment I am talking about. A veritable solstice of silence filled the room. The linguistic interpretation of "sleep with me" as opposed to, say, "share the larger bed," threw a hush over the testosterone-tempered group.

The strange quiet begged for a logical resolution. But, alas, the young men were smitten. In other less awkward circumstances, which any man would recognize and respond to if he stumbled upon them alone, the four beleaguered guys might have fought to the death to sleep with the beautiful Joanna. Instead, as a group they timidly told her, "No, this is fine," and for her to enjoy her night alone in the huge bed.

Now, looking back, I am confident that *that* moment is indelibly etched into the maleness of those four young guys. In the years to come their private thoughts and dreams will play out different resolutions of that situation.

It's just part of being a guy.

Tragic Tour

I inwardly smiled to myself as the motor coach raced by the J. and J. Restaurant on our way to Denali National Park. It had been exactly a year since I had done my last tour #4, yet the memories were still fresh in my mind of my encounters with Adolph, Eva, and the 50, tattooed waiter in the REDRUM tee shirt.

I only had 22 guests with me on this year's amended version of tour #4. The tour now included box lunches prepared by our train crew in Anchorage. The box lunch included a turkey slice in a croissant bun, an apple, a package of potato chips, two Oreo cookies, and a nine ounce bottle of Pure Alaskan Water. This food proved to be quite satisfying to the guests, but to lose out on the inevitable drama that would be created by a stop at J. and J. (With it's infinite permutations and combinations of food items such as last year's Buffalo Burgers, Musk Ox Burgers, Salmon Patties, cole slaw, and potato salad.) Well, I just had to sigh and feel as though I were somehow cheating the guests.

This group of 22 guests included a family of 20, plus one other couple who, very good-naturedly, accepted their fate of being a de facto member of the Miles clan for four days. This group of assorted Miles struck me as being a traveling poster child for the true definition of dysfunctional families.

The Patriarch of this family was Howard Miles Jr., who was in charge of the total preparation of this family vacation; which he willingly paid for every five years. Howard Junior was 76-year-old and sat by himself in the front of the motor coach. Traveling with him were his two sons and one daughter, along with 16 variations of in-laws and grandchildren, including Howard Miles III and Howard Miles IV. I rarely witnessed the three siblings involved in anything but guarded conversations and the only people who seemed to be enjoying each other were the teenaged and early 20s grandchildren. Even with them there existed a definite pecking order. None of the family seemed interested in anything I had to say.

A 74-year-old, left handed man and his equally aged wife traveled north on the same road as our motor coach and were approximately 60 miles ahead of us, as my driver Fred and I tried our best to entertain our enigmatic guests. The man and his wife had flown into Anchorage that morning, rented a car, and were heading to Denali National Park. The couple had friends who came to Alaska on a tour such as ours the previous summer, and they believed that they could save money by doing the driving themselves.

Thus far, Howard Miles Jr. had walked down the aisle of the motor coach and distributed 20 dollar bills to the other 19 family members. I surmised that this must be a daily ritual, since nobody seemed to protest or thank him. He had boasted to me that he was on the Winter Olympic Committee, had spoken several times with Alaska's senior senator, Ted Stevens, had already charged $60,000 onto his credit card, had been at a dinner with the first astronauts who had walked on the moon, had been on a bobsled run in Utah when he was 70 years old, and was the owner of luxury hotels in South Carolina and Hawaii. I could probably fill another page with other boasts of property and experiences Howard Miles Jr. shared with me during our three days together at the front of the motor coach—but I won't.

I remember an interview with Richard Nixon several years after he was forced from office. In reference to all of the fund raising parties he was forced to attend as president,he said, "I hated these dinners with wealthy influence grabbers. These people spouted endlessly about themselves and their possessions. They could never see how horribly boring they really were!" Sitting beside Howard Miles Jr. made me recall that Nixon interview and realize what a simplistic notion wealth and power was.

Heading south on the same highway were six men, traveling in single file on large motorcycles. They had begun their trip of a lifetime three weeks earlier from a town in northeast Ohio. They reached their turn around point in Fairbanks yesterday and were pleased because they were a day ahead of their schedule. The fourth man in the single file of motorcycles traveling at 65 miles an hour had been the mastermind of this journey. He had convinced the other five members of this motorcycle group a year earlier. They had all retired from the fire house where he was still employed. (He had seen too many people die soon after retirement and wanted this trip to revitalize his buddies.) Two years of saving vacation days and pleading with his wife were responsible for his presence.

" What's this crap all about?" my 67-year-old impatient driver Fred said as he had to grind our motor coach to a halt a few miles north of Trapper Creek. We could see a couple hundred yards ahead of us to the left a group of people with binoculars who had exited their vehicles and were staring ahead from a bend in the road. A helicopter zoomed over our vehicle as we came to a stop. Obviously, some type of accident had happened and it would delay our getting to our lunch location of Veteran's Memorial, which was still around 30 miles ahead of us.

Fred, the driver, radioed ahead to the motor coach that was traveling with us on tour #4. "It looks pretty bad," David, the other driver responded to our questioning.

That was enough of a response for me to break out the box lunches for the guests. I also announced that I thought that on this clear section of straight highway, an accident might have occurred by someone falling asleep.

It was a beautiful day so the Miles poured off of the motor coach and ran around picking newly blooming fireweed. I asked the most shunned of the sons, David, who had the misfortune of not being named Howard, if he enjoyed these vacations every five years.

He looked at me blandly and with no emotion elicited this response. "What do you think?" and turned away. End of conversation. Obviously, most of the Miles endured these half decade vacations to stay in good favor with their wildly wealthy father/grandfather.

It was an hour later that the traffic once again began to move.

It was two days later that the scene we were all about to witness was described in the newspaper. It seemed that the 74-year-old man's wife had a pillow and was propped up against the window asleep. The man who had wanted to save money fell asleep. Although the new indentations on each side of the highway were there to save his wife and him should this occurrence happen, the man was left handed, so the dominant hand drifted the car across the median and into our group of six firemen on motorcycles. The first motorcycle was already past the drifting mid-sized rental and the second motorcycle only had to veer slightly to miss a collision. The third cyclist missed the car by inches, but the fourth motorcyclist, the man who had organized this trip, was adjusting his helmet as all of this was taking place and hit the car directly in the middle. In a split second the man woke up and veered back to the right. Unfortunately, the fifth cyclist adjusted his course to the left to miss the car and he also hit the car head on because of the car's adjustment. The sixth cyclist was able to lay his motorcycle down and slid past the carnage into the willow trees. He and his motorcycle had only minor damage. In an instant the book was closed on the lives of the fourth and fifth motorcyclists. Their trip of a lifetime had ended tragically and the four survivors would fly with their friend's caskets back to Ohio. The older couple survived because of the air bags installed on the later modeled rental car.

When the tour bus number 114 reached the accident scene, all aboard became silent as we saw the burned out carcass of the white Ford rental car. Both motorcycles must have struck the car directly in the middle since the front of the vehicle was crushed nearly halfway to the windshield.

I sighed and realized that nobody on a motorcycle could have lived through such a collision. I looked around seeking some sort of emotional empathy from the guests and caught Howard Miles Junior's eyes.

"I've had dinner with the president of Harley Davidson," he said proudly.

'What an idiot' I thought as the hum from the self-important Mile's resumed behind me a minute after we passed the accident scene.

Elitism

I was standing at the top of the cement stairs at Denali Park's train depot scanning the area for one last guest who had inexplicably needed to "take a walk." Odd behavior, yes. But, at the mid point of the season, when workers in the tourism business consider bolting, and thus losing the 10% bonus, that comes with lasting the entire 16 weeks, very little seems odd.

I sighed at last, when I spotted Mr. McCabe walking briskly toward us. I figured, incorrectly, that he simply had to find a bathroom in the terminal, to alleviate a dire need.

I had luckily drawn the *split group* assignment on this breakfast leg from Fairbanks to Denali. My instructions were to divide my 43 guests into two even groups and in so doing give each car an equal number of people to serve. The beauty of this role was that I could stay the majority amount of the time on the train car that harbored the crew of six whose sanity was least compromised at this juncture of the season. I would walk between both train cars. On this Tuesday morning I had stayed 90% of the time in the back train car, thus, if some other reason had caused Mr. McCabe's delay, I wouldn't be privy to it.

This group of 43 seemed much less threatening than my group from the previous week. There was only one group of eight people from Wisconsin who were traveling together. They laughed, seemingly, all the time, so, as long as I kept from being the brunt of their humor, they seemed easily manageable.

Getting to the McKinley Village Lodge finally at 9 PM (After a mind numbing eight hour school bus ride of 120 miles on a gravel road—with a reasonably insane guide named Jewel.) I passed out the room keys, went to my room to freshen up, and then sought some sustenance.

The bar at McKinley Village was packed, so I headed across the parking lot to a competitor's restaurant, named The Road House. The Road House was always less crowded, but getting your food order through to the English language challenged foreign workers was sometimes similar to the old BBC television show *Fawlty Towers* where the hotel owner, John Cleese, was always trying to communicate with his Spanish speaking only waiter Miguel. (All of the business establishments in Denali were only opened from mid-May till mid-September. Hiring foreign workers who would happily work at minimum wage on four month working visas was the avenue most employers took.)

I walked in and spotted the McCabes, who were sitting at a two place table and who were waving me over. "Why don't you have a seat with us?" Mr. McCabe offered and I grabbed a chair.

"We can't seem to get anyone's attention to place an order. All we want are cheeseburgers and cokes," an exasperated Mrs. McCabe said.

I motioned to a nervous looking Miguel whom, although facing only half a dozen filled tables, seemed overwhelmed.

"Yes?" Miguel said while looking around for help.

"We would like three cheeseburgers."

"I…not…order…taker," Miguel said and started to walk away.

"Wait!" I insisted and quickly wrote our order on a napkin and handed it to Miguel, "Take this back to the cook, he'll understand."

"We probably have about a fifty-percent chance of getting our order," I told the McCabe's who seemed to be amused about the situation, after I explained the working conditions to them. We three began to munch on the crackers that were at the table in the event that no food would be forth-coming.

We briefly talked about our great fortune at being able to see a large female grizzly and her three cubs close to the road on our trip into Denali Park. Then Mr. McCabe suddenly said; "I bet you are wondering, Fred, why I was late to board the motor coach."

I shook my head to the negative as I savored the last cracker on the table.

"Well, we sat behind two ladies from that group of eight and well; they just never stopped talking for four straight hours. They would laugh loudly over the most inane topics, that were in no way funny. Then to top it off we were seated with them for breakfast. I had to walk around to try and get my sanity back."

"Yes, that seems like a basic sort of group." I responded knowing that both McCabe and his wife were professors at a huge university in Northern Texas.

"We knew that it is a roll of the dice with whom you end up with on tours like this, but that certainly tested our patience," McCabe said and both he and his wife laughed as suddenly three cheeseburgers arrived.

"Boy, that's fast service," I said, inwardly wondering how many hours these may have been sitting back there.

We all attacked the food. (The box snack offered on the eight hour trip into the park was hardly filling.)

"I hate to sound elitist, Fred," McCabe said between bites, but could you help us to be separated from that boorish group for the rest of the trip?"

I wondered if I held some elitist attitude, since I also had been avoiding this group. My reasoning was based upon my first interaction with Dexter, one of the male leaders of this group of eight, who approached me while I was loading luggage at River's Edge Hotel in Fairbanks, sixteen hours earlier.

"Hey Fred. I just had back surgery five weeks before this trip. Let me show you my scar," Dexter said and before I could object, he had turned around, lifted his shirt and pulled down his pants to an area that gave me full view of a six inch scar that ran along his lower spinal chord, but also gave me a view of at least three inches of his rear cleavage. What sickened me most was viewing an alien tuft of black hair that grew just above the cleavage.

"Oh lord," I heard myself say, and then complimented him on how tough he was to come on a trip so shortly after an operation.

I kept the McCabe's away from the Wisconsin group the last three days and I wondered if we should start training new tour directors to attempt social segregation.

With a growing number of guided tours, 23% of all Alaska travelers, it may be as important to typecast the groups beforehand— or not.

Boy Band and the Trillionaires

Boy Band's expression of excitement was infectious, as he told two thirds of *The Perfect Storm* (This nicknamed group is generally Karen, Dani, and Julie. But this week Missy took Karen's place.) and myself about his ideal future with six of his guests, whom earlier in the week had informed him that their personal wealth was beyond comprehension by mere mortals.

We four tour directors sat in the back of the lower deck on the

The Perfect Storm

Riverboat Discovery III as the boat made its way toward Chena Village, having just witnessed Dixie Alexander fillet an eleven pound Chum salmon in a minute and four seconds.

I wanted to slap Boy Band back to reality, but since it was only a third of the way into the season in his first year as a tour director, I simply smiled; he would learn.

We four were on the final day of a five day tour, so we had already endured four days of Boy Band's excited rantings. Two thirds of the Perfect Storm and I had attempted to temper Boy

Band's assured prognosis that his new relationship with the trillionaires was going to lead to a life of leisure.

Without exception, the guests we meet each summer, whom choose to share their personal wealth either through displays or through verbosity with their tour director, reveal their true ingenuous nature before parting.

Boy Band's privileged group of six included a set of siblings and their spouses—plus a pair of obnoxiously spoiled eleven-year-old male offspring. The younger ones had informed Boy Band that they owned an island in Central America and that it cost six hundred dollars in helicopter fees just to get to their tropical estate. The older ones threw into this story the fact that this island retreat remained empty much of the year and that Boy Band could live there free of charge anytime he wished—also, that they knew so many people down there who could set him up as a diver or touring agent to other super-rich people.

"Yeah, I'm set for life!" Boy Band beamed—as the alpha male of the group approached him and with his index finger indicated that he wished to speak to him in private.

This was a typical M.O. all week for the trillionaires—expecting and receiving special treatment from Boy Band—although there were another 30 guests with his group.

Boy Band

A few minutes later Boy Band came back with even less color in his face that his Dutch heritage had already given him. "They are bored—they want to take a taxi out of Chena Village."

Two thirds of The Perfect Storm laughed, but I knew that there was a way to get off this supposed island—having had an ill guest taxied off of here the year before. What surprised us was the fact that they were not enjoying this experience. In the previous 80 or so groups I had taken onto this beautiful riverboat, I had found maybe two souls who showed ill humor at this three and a half hour tour on the Chena and Tanana Rivers.

We found Phil, the riverboat's award winning commentator, and had him phone a taxi, so that the trillionaires might escape this merely mortal experience.

We didn't say anything to Boy Band about his elitist guests, but we couldn't help but notice that uncertainty was creeping onto the 23-year-old face, that only a few minutes earlier had displayed a secure passage into the trillionaire's world.

The next morning, I flew to Anchorage with one third of The Perfect Storm, thus I wasn't privy to how Boy Band's mini-gold seeking drama played out—until later, when I was able to speak with another third of The Perfect Storm.

Danielle, who goes by Dani this season and is undoubtedly the  strongest low pressure system of The Perfect Storm, informed me that as both groups waited at Gate 4 at the Fairbanks Airport for their flight back to Anchorage. Boy Band opened some of his tip envelopes—especially the one that held the tips from the six trillionaires. He found only two, 20 dollar bills in the envelope. It should have contained $15 per person—or $90 total, which explained why the trillionaires were now ignoring Boy Band.

Dani noticed the near suicidal look on Boy Band's face and walked to him holding a hundred dollar bill in one of her hands, that two of her couples had combined together to give her. She was with a group of square dancers from Arkansas whom I had labeled 'Dosi-No Dough' indicating that they would probably be light tippers.

"Look what I received from one of my couples!" Dani said, so that the two spoiled 11-year-olds, who stood a few yards away, could see.

Boy Band looked even more distressed and had no response for Dani, who then watched as the two brats ran to the alpha male, who acquired more cash, which they then brought back to Boy Band.

Boy Band looked a bit relieved, but realized that he had been played for sucker all week and had learned a valuable life lesson.

The Roberta Effect

I am sure we have all encountered folks we notice have a pattern in their lives, whether that be the preponderance or the lack of good fortune, a tendency toward good or ill health, or even the gift of coming up with or inability to find the perfect words in life's situations. I call these tendencies. Last season in the tour directing world in Alaska, I detected a tendency with one of our tour directors.

Several odd occurrences took place in the witness of Roberta. This cute 22-year-old from Palmer, Alaska had proven to be an extremely successful tour director. Her wit, confidence, and style easily won over even the most ornery of groups—but strange happenings were taking place, a bit too often.

For example; on her second tour, Roberta was walking through the motor coach handing out tags for the guests to add to their bags, which they would find in their first hotel room. She did this effortlessly as the bus whizzed toward Talkeetna. When she got to the rear of the vehicle she noticed that the newlywed couple was involved in a state of activity—heavy kissing and petting was taking place and the woman was nude from the waist up. Roberta had to say "I'm coming back in 10 minutes with info I will need from you. You better have your clothes on!

On a subsequent tour, Roberta had a man on her tour from

Spain who spoke little English. This strange, dark haired, man had a unique problem. He refused to use the toilet that is located at the back of each motor coach. Instead, he would get off of the coach each time they would stop, even in downtown Anchorage, go to the back corner of the coach, open his pants, and relieve himself in public. Roberta labeled him TPU (The Public Urinator).

She also had a middle-aged married couple swear to divorce each other after the tour ended—in an ugly yelling match on the motor coach.

A near race riot broke out when a group of southern white racist types were inexplicably blended with two black families, whom happened to reside in a neighboring county.

These sort of situations probably are deemed to occur whenever you throw 28,000 guests into 52 different motor

Roberta

coaches in a 16 week period—but for the most outrageous events to take place with one woman, the same woman—well, that requires a title: The Roberta Effect.

Menopause Tour

The first five weeks of tour directing has been fairly slow as far as stories go. My mainstay Roberta, formerly known as, The Effect, used to give me weekly odd occurrences to report upon. She no longer wants that moniker after a $5k engine problem driving up here to Alaska.

Heidi had a first tour called the New Delhi No Tippers.

Celia just finished a burst hemorrhoid tour (BHT)—if you want details—ask her!

Lance had another group of trillionaires who tipped him five dollars each—some things never change.

Stephanie Campo, a tour director at Premier had a dozen guests, women wearing diamonds, rush from the Denali River Cabins to the parking lot at The Village yelling at her with scrunched up faces, "They have run out of food tat the restaurant!"

But the best story I've heard so far is Adam's Menopause Tour, of which I have only heard brief details. But, of course, truth has never played a big part of my story telling, so here goes.

Adam is one of the most kind of our tour directors. He genuinely cares for his guests and seems to have a continual laugh emanating from his being. I have even suggested to him that should a guest reveal to him that they were dying from terminal cancer he would respond, "Ha. Ha. Oh, that's too bad. But hey, we're all going to die anyway, ha, ha."

With this brief introduction, I give to you Adam on his Menopause Tour. Adam found himself eating pot roast in the bar at the Talkeetna Alaskan Lodge when Christina, a tour director paralleling him, and my daughter, motioned to him with a sly grin to come toward the lobby. He could tell by her look that something was up. What Adam saw made him laugh—but it wasn't a laugh of humor. It was a laugh based upon nervousness.

Wanda, a dark-haired, mid-40s, heavy set woman, who was on his tour was sitting on one of the plush couches next to the 40-foot-high stone fireplace and was putting a serious lip-lock on John, one of the pilots for an airtaxi service in Talkeetna. A problem arose from this situation, which Stephanie Campo said was a scene no tour director needs to see. Wanda's husband, Mitchell, was sitting back in the bar knocking down his second Long Island Iced Tea. Adam's further disbelief stemmed from the fact that the night before in the lobby of the Grande Denali Lodge, Mitchell had caught his wife kissing a man she had met on the cruise ship five days earlier. That event ended with Mitchell calmly asking Wanda to stop kissing the man and come to the room with him.

Her response was, f...you!" She wiped some spit from her mouth, "I'll come to bed when I'm good and ready!"

Adam wasn't married and couldn't understand what appeal this woman had over these other men. Wanda wasn't that attractive, but had a nice figure. It was when she drank (She had two Vodka 7s before leaving Mitchell at the bar.) that seemed to allow her amorous side to take over.

Adam decided to deal with this predicament as most seasoned tour directors would—he immediately retreated to his room.

Amazingly, Wanda decided to share with him what had happened to her the previous night as Mitchell and she were boarding the motor coach the next day. Evidently, John the pilot (We later learned that John was a desperately lonely Talkeetna full time resident.) had flown Wanda with him later that evening and landed on a glacier, at base camp for all of the climbers of Mt. McKinley.

Adam on an excursion with his guests the week before.

"It was amazing!" Wanda laughed, with vodka breath nearly gagging Adam and pinched him on the butt.

Adam shook his head as he was boarding the motor coach realizing that Wanda had now had probably given a whole new meaning to the word *base* camp!

One Early September Day in Fairbanks

Two ravens, the keepers of the north country, spiraled down-ward in an aerial dance above the Fairbanks Airport toward two newly arrived bright, shiny objects. The objects of the raven's attention were two private jets parked at the edge of the tarmac. These representatives of society's wealth were posing at such an angle so that the trucks and cars that passed nearby could amply appreciate their splendor.

Stationed between the road and these duo objects of admiration sat a narrow resplendent field of fireweed, whose reddish, purple blooms had now reached their peak of brilliance. This sea of magenta reminded those living in this northern land that summer was quickly coming to an end. In a week, this strikingly beautiful plant, that defines Alaska for two months each year, will turn bright red and distribute cotton-like seeds throughout the Alaskan skies and thus redefine the land the next July.

The jets had brought two billionaires above 64 degrees N. Latitude for a purpose less exuberant than a late summer vacation. They had come to attend a memorial for a famous dog musher. The billionaires had befriended the dog musher after success and distinction had brought her onto the world's stage.

The billionaire's world and the world of the dog musher could not have presented more of a juxtaposition—yet there in a smallish auditorium they sat listening attentively to other dog mushers share personal anecdotes and compassionate stories from the trail. They sat as the dog musher's husband talked lovingly of his now departed partner in life, while his now motherless daughters sat in front of him on the stage. Tears flowed—but not from the billionaire's eyes.

The two ravens now sat in a tree outside the window of the auditori-um. Their steel, black-eyed gaze seemed to sense that there was something amiss in the world of humans. Then, inexplicably, the billionaires each got up and spoke of their personal interactions with the newly deceased dog musher. The local people listened, but not really. They knew that shortly the private jets at the airport would whisk these strangers back to a world from which the dog musher had long ago turned her back—as had many Alaskans.

It was a kind gesture that the billionaires had chosen to attend the memorial—it displayed to we Alaskans how one woman's achievements can affect all types of people. But, I seriously doubt that, as the billionaires went to sleep on their four hour flight back south, whether they could conceive of the extent to which this dog musher had, in her brief time in the north country, touched the heart of what truly *is* Alaska.

Once all of the humans had left the auditorium, the ravens once again took to the sky. They soared over the Chena and Tanana Rivers. The dogs at the dog musher's kennel barked at them and they both looked down at the stick nest nestled on a cliff next to the glacial river, where they had raised four new chicks earlier in the summer.

The Art of Giving

In the tour directing business, the power of giving exerts its being from each moment to each moment.

> ...in a society... it is the giving and receiving and giving in return, that makes our lives pleasant and harmonious. But woe to the receiver who gives nothing in return; who is so wrapped up in himself/herself that he/she has no idea that his/her non-action blocks the flow of kindness and love that otherwise would have come to his/her aid in a time of need.
>
> *Eloise Hart*

This past week, my wife, Cecilia, had two guests out of 51 on our beloved Tour #12, whom had no clue about the karmic value of giving. They each found petty issues to complain about and attempted to sway the positive energy of love and giving which both Celia and I try to promote to our groups, as we show off this beautiful northern land.

For six days her group had to endure the frowns and negative conversations of these two people—yet while witnessing the beauty of a pack of howling wolves, moose, caribou, and dall sheep in Denali Park, the majesty of Mt. McKinley as they flew over it, and the honesty of Cecilia as she passed around artifacts and shared stories about her 32 years living in this beautiful country.

But, is it just these two lost souls or do each of us somehow lose track of the power of giving from time to time?

I always remember a scene from one of my favorite movies *Groundhog Day*. In this scene Bill Murray is suddenly running down a sidewalk and catches a young boy who falls from a tree.

"You have never thanked me!" Bill Murray says in an exasperated tone of voice as the young boy runs away. Yet Murray still shows up at this exact time each day to give the gift of non-injury to this young person. For those not familiar with this movie, the arrogant and self serving big city weatherman, Bill Murray is evidently doomed to relive the same day, Groundhog Day, for eternity—or at least until he gets it right.

I think that all of us occasionally allow negativity and non-action to occur where it shouldn't occur—we don't give of ourselves, as we should. We look too hard for others to give to us.

Life just doesn't work that way!

Shel Silverstein wrote this beautiful kid's book called *The Giving Tree*. I used to make all my 4th and 5th graders read it—then we'd act it out and I'd then send three or four kids around to the other classrooms to show it off.

The story is about an apple tree that give and gives and gives to a young boy who ages and continues to take and take and take until the tree simply has nothing left to give. The tree understands the power of giving. At the end of the book it seems that the boy does also.

Celia said her goodbyes to the two difficult guests by shaking their hands at the airport in Anchorage before they boarded the motor coach to Seward. Both looked away, not wishing to look her in the eyes. There were no gratuities coming from these people.

But, as tour directors, we should always be there to 'catch them' as Bill Murray did—it's what we do!

Making an Effort

I've read a couple biographies the past few weeks that reinforce my feelings concerning humanity and the roles Celia and I play in our summer employment as Alaska tour directors. Those feelings revolve around the notion that each of us carry an award winning novel within the vicissitudes of our lives. It simply takes an ability of perception to notice it.

The first biography is called *Mockingbird* by Charles J. Shields. I picked this book, written in 2006, because it chronicled the life of Nelle Harper Lee, the author of one of my favorite books/movies *To Kill a Mockingbird*. What I learned about Lee was that this is her only novel, that she is a loner to the extreme, never married and still lives in Monroeville, Alabama. She grants no interviews and gave Mr. Shields no assistance in his biography, which he based upon more than 600 separate interviews with people associated with Ms. Lee. She is presently 82 years old and bears a resemblance to many of the older women who come on Alaska cruise tours.

The beauty of her novel is that it is based upon the people and events in her small town in Alabama in the 1930s and 40s. Not unlike Mark Twain's *Tom Sawyer*, she paints a picture of a very simple way of life—yet within this simplicity resides intricate personalities shading the landscape both positively and negatively. This intricate labyrinth of interpersonal relationships resides in all of us. We choose sometimes to suppress much of the meaningful aspects of the fabric that has made each of us into the personalities now standing before us.

Why don't we make efforts to find out more or accept more about ourselves?

Maybe, because if we lived each day considering all of the possibilities, injustices, maltreatment, and sheer good and bad fortune that has confronted each of us—our chances for a non-schizophrenic society might be even more remote than they presently are.

There was a moment in young Nelle Lee's life that leads me to describe to you the second book I recently read.

One early evening, as a young tomboy of 10 years of age she and her friend Truman Capote heard the snapping of a branch in a fenced in lot—they both found knotholes in the fence to peer through and saw a young black man hanging by the neck from a branch that had snapped from the force. A group of half a dozen white people stood around and the young kids heard this comment before they both fled. "That were just 'bout a near purfect hangin'—he dun died right off!"

I sat in the ninth row-seat D on our flight back to Anchorage on tour #12 a few weeks back. Beside me in seats E and F were Harold Lash and his wife Edith from Toronto, Canada. They were both in their mid-80s and I had to watch out for them all week, but Mrs. Lash had fallen at the Fairbanks Airport, so I was glad I had been placed next to them on this particular flight—for further reassurance that she was alright.

Harold and I talked. His whisper-like voice (from a stroke a few years back) was difficult to make out from the drone of the jet engines. He told me how Edith had saved his life during that illness and that this was their first trip since then. He also told me that he was a retired policeman of 35 years in the Toronto area. I then asked him if he ever felt in danger.

"No, I was fortunate, I guess. But, I had a brother who was shot and killed by a mean man. I got my brother the police job. He left four young kids behind. I've always felt bad about that," he hesitated and then went on. "They hung that mean man. He was the last man hung in Canada, before they got rid of capital punishment."

When I got home I Googled Lash and 'last man hung' and found a recently published book called *The Last to Die* by Robert J. Hoshowsky. The book talks of two men Arthur Lucas, an accused murderer from Detroit and Ronald Turpin, the man accused of killing Harold Lash's brother. The book discusses both the sad, desperate road that led these men to the gallows one cold December night in 1962 and the barbarous nature of the hanging industry. Evidently, one of the men was not a purfect hangin.'

The book is well written and I found out much more about the two people I sat with for 42 minutes between Fairbanks and Anchorage, Alaska.

I had made an effort—and found out more.

Rooms With a View

Whenever one of our land tours see Mt. McKinley in Denali Park on their Tundra Wilderness Tour or their Denali Natural History Tour and then heads south to Talkeetna, there will be a few guests who will be upset when they don't get a room with a view. This was once again the case on Tour #6 this past week. It is always interesting to me to witness both the amount of duress the guests express and the logic that they use as to why *they* should be given special privileges over the other score of people, whom also did not receive rooms with a view.

This aspect of human nature has me considering how we all prejudice our perceptions in the visual area. We own at least four other senses, yet we live most of our lives depending upon the notion, *if we can see it, we can believe it.*

Allow me to describe a situation that happened in my second season as a tour director, also in Denali National Park, that made me feel that we indeed need to look to other aspects of our being besides just the ocular. But first, this quote seems appropriate;

Pointing the Way
There is a sanctuary, to which the mind may journey when the outer self grows weary of the seemingly

endless chain of worldly activities....as closely and naturally as a heartbeat to the life is the ingress to the heart of being linked to the mind and outer nature.

An aura of inspiration marks the vicinity of entrance, a subtle soundless breath, a radiant power which is ceaselessly poured out from the heart of being; this is the neighborhood of the inner god...

Can one point the way to that sanctuary? Devotion, the constant effort of the outer person to serve all that lives—joy in that service and in sacrifice to the lesser self: these are our signposts, our unerring guides.

G. W. Hockinson

I found myself at the turnaround spot on the Denali Natural History Tour. The group I was accompanying was small; a mix of a dozen couples; mostly from the midwest. These people had not seemed overly impressed with their afternoon trip into the park. We had seen a lone bull moose thus far and Mount McKinley had been shrouded in clouds. Even though we advertise this shorter tour as a history of the park tour—guests still expect to see all of the animals.

"Follow me!" our Athabascan Indian guide Jenny announced when everyone had disembarked the converted school bus. She took us to the southern point of the rest area and had us face north. Our young driver, Aaron, accompanied us and whispered in my ear, "Your guests will like Jenny. She's new here."

Jenny stood on a small hill facing us and began explaining to us how this Denali region was sacred hunting grounds for her people and how this *Mother Earth* will take care of all people if you'll let it!

She then seemed to change her manner as she looked over our heads and shouted! "Do not under any circumstances turn around! Close your eyes and listen as I bear this drum my great grandfather beat for me!" She then began to chant and beat her skin drum. I looked around and saw that everyone had their eyes closed—so I closed mine.

"We are one with Mother Earth. Put your fingers to your wrists. Keep your eyes closed. Count the beats of your heart. It is now the same as the beat of my great grandfather's drum."

My skin began to tingle as I realized that my heartbeat was mimicking the beat of her drum.

"This beat is not just from my drum It's coming from our beautiful earth. Now slowly turn around and open your eyes."

We all did as instructed and before us stood a now perfectly clear Mt. McKinley—dominating the pristine landscape. Many of the people then began to cry and, even I, must admit to some watering in my eyes.

Jenny had taken all of us *beyond* simply the visual.

The Kiss

Having just completed the training for my eighth season as tour director, I must admit that I kept a fairly low profile this year. Maybe it was because the company hired more than 50 new tour directors, drivers, and train personnel. Whenever there is a year of sizable turnover there tends to be an overabundance of zeal. Now zeal is okay, in small portions, but this "we've hired the best so and so's ever," really pales on the reality scale in Fred's world. The reality being that we have no idea how these new people will stand up under the pressure of 17 straight weeks of long hours of daily responsibilities.

I've noticed, over the years, that a certain trend seems to present itself. For the first seven or eight weeks situations tend to progress reasonably well—having the incredible product of Alaska scenery and unique experiences pulls the new employees into the excited world of the guests—but then from about week eight until maybe week 11 this psychology seems to break down. A *hitting of the wall* occurs because of fatigue and in many employees their A game is replaced by a B- or a C+ game. Finally, a *mental sigh* occurs around week 12, as we all see that the end is approaching and reasonable state of normalcy returns.

It was around week 10 a few years back that I met Maye and

Bertha. Whenever the manifest lists names like these or Elmer, Clyde, Orville, etc. you are assured that these guests will be in their 70s. They were really delightful ladies from the midwest whom had each recently lost their husbands and decided to come to Alaska together. We were on tour #12 together and they had continually complimented our company and me for the wonderful experiences they were having. And I had to admit I was a bit sad to see them leave, as I was saying my goodbyes at the International Airport in Anchorage.

Maye and Bertha were among the last to load onto the motor coach which would then take them to their cruise ship in Seward. Because of my fatigue, I was standing a bit closer to the guests than I generally do. Bertha had given me a hug and Ewing, their driver, was helping her onto the bus.

I could see that Maye was pursing her lips as she leaned toward me, but our heads were advancing at similar trajectories and at the last moment we turned our heads the same way and suddenly I was giving a full lip kiss to a 75 year old woman. Now, polite kisses last but a moment, yet I couldn't seem to escape from this red lip-sticked, thickly made up faced, heavily perfumed experience. She smiled as she finally pulled away and I saw that the driver Ewing was laughing at me. I had a flood of emotions in those milli seconds." What just happened? Did that kiss mean something more? Should I follow Maye on board and het her phone number?

Well, its been a couple of years, but I still look for the name Maye on every manifest.

Incident on the Train

"Roughage! Roughage! Why won't anyone eat roughage!" Missy announced in an animated way as she stuck her head through the, air pressure controlled, sliding door and faced Crystal and myself. The three of us, as tour directors, had patiently awaited until our 112 guests had finished their breakfast, and now sat awaiting the delivery of our ordered carbohydrate-laced, artery filling enticements.

Missy

We, our guests, and the six train employees were aboard our train car—the most luxurious train car in the world. Built to specifications, for our company by an outfit in Ft. Lupton, Colorado, that made each train car one inch longer and one inch higher than any of the competition. Each of the 80 leather seats in the domed upper section had cost the company $1,500 and were rated the highest in comfort.

I shook my head as we raced northward through Wasilla, at 45 miles per hour, wondering why Missy needed to get into the rest-room to wash her hands for the third time that morning. It seemed to me that many of both the tour directors and motor coach drivers had a reasonable obsession toward cleansing their cuticles.

"Sit down Missy," I demanded, "One less hand washing session won't bring on the Norwalk Disease."

Missy begrudgingly acquiesced as Steve Kaiser, our server, somehow managed to bring all three of our orders without dropping anything, as the train car bounced from side to side.

"There are people in those two bathrooms who have been in there *way* too long!" Missy said, still upset that she couldn't wash her hands.

Missy was a fun loving, late-20s beauty who had just begun tour directing this season. She had been a guest service representative (GSR) at the Marriott Hotel in Anchorage the previous season and was an elementary school teacher during the winter. Ironically, she and I shared an experience a few years earlier when she was teaching in the Athabascan Indian village of McGrath, while I was substituting in the Eskimo/Indian village of Holy Cross. I huddled in the room that was provided for me in the winter of 2002 (The same room where the blanket on my bed froze to the wall one minus 40 plus degree night.) listening to the only radio station coming into the village. That radio station emanated from McGrath and it was Missy doing the DJ work.

We had just begun to devour the omelets, blueberry pancakes, and cranberry scones, when a shortish man sporting a drawn down baseball cap over a more than likely balding head, stuck his head through the now permanently opened sliding door and announced in a drawl that could be heard by the two other tables of guests. "Some dudes gunna have to do something. That larger bathroom's crapper isn't flushing. I'm tellin' ya folks—there's one large load in there."

Crystal, Missy, and I put down our forks just as the stench of the man's verbal reality hit our noses. "Crystal—hit the switch," Missy and I yelled at the same time.

Crystal stood on her tiptoes and pushed the toggle switch down—which closed the door. I turned to see the disgusted looks on the eight people's faces who had chosen to stay downstairs. They quickly made their way back upstairs, while holding their noses.

Steve Kaiser quickly located Pablo, the Consist Manager for both train cars, and with a look of determination, Pablo, carrying a strange looking black valise, plodded into the vile pit of perpetration. The three of us had somehow lost our appetites, but kept sipping on our glasses of juice and coffee as we awaited the outcome of our newest set of circumstances.

"Well, that has been taken care of," Pablo announced, ten minutes later, as he slid in beside Crystal at our table.

"What was in that black case you took into there?" I asked.

"A laptop computer," Pablo laughed, "Those vacuum toilets get out of synch and are computer controlled."

"There's a software program for our software?" I joked.

"And our hardware," Pablo joked back.

There was a moment of silence and then Pablo, a veteran of three years on these train cars continued; "You know, I always tell myself that when I go in there to fix this problem that I won't look into the stool. It really is a simple process…but…" he hesitated and looked up expressing a sense of arcane melancholy, "I always look. I sprayed, so it should be back to normal in a few minutes," Pablo said in a business sort of way.

Pablo then left and I was left alone to ponder what it was that he had seen, or if I would have looked, and if at least on this morning, if in fact, I could get back to *normal*.

Goodall Observes N.J. Sisters

Have you heard of Jane Goodall? She is a famous anthropologist who has spent the majority of her life living amongst, and studying, the life styles of the wild chimpanzees of Africa. Being 55 years of age, I have been subjected to television, magazine, and newspaper articles about her life and the perceptions she has happened upon, because of her time with these supposedly wild animals. I have always enjoyed the way in which she would name each of her chimpanzees and thus, through the use of personification, align personality traits and create a social illusion for her and the people for whom she would report her findings. Although, I always attempted to take Jane's discoveries seriously, I couldn't get past the mental visualization that she was a desperately lonely woman with something of a monkey fetish, who at high school prom probably had to play Clue in the kitchen, while all of her supposed friends were making out in the living room.

Anyway, Tour 6A was a tour this year where I assumed a Jane Goodall approach to the reality. I noted on my clip board (all anthropologists must have a clip board) that it was on this date the previous season that I had my encounter with the Howard Miller IV family of 22. So, I noted this seasonal synchronicity when I met the 16 members of the Catz family. There were seven adults and nine offspring who varied in ages from three to 19. They were from New Jersey and Florida. (When you direct tours you quickly learn that Florida is simply a euphemism for people originally from New Jersey and New York.)

This group was originally supposed to be 18 in number, but the parents of the mid-aged adults feigned illness and wisely backed out at the last minute. This left the dominance of this tribe in question and when I walked into Pike's Waterfront Lodge in Fairbanks at 11 AM on Monday July 19th, I immediately became the focus of this power struggle.

There were four middle-aged sisters. All about five feet four inches in height. All wearing blouses that did not cover midriffs (that should have been covered) and white pants that only extended halfway down their calves. Three of the sisters were black haired and had brought along offspring and husbands. I mention offspring before husbands because from the start, it was obvious to this reporter that the attention the young humans received was far in excess to the husbands, who received mostly scorn and manipulation. The other female was divorced and after spending five days with *Bleach-Blond Little Monkey-Face*, I have no doubts that there exists a shallow grave, somewhere in New Jersey which contains the remains of the poor soul that chose this alpha female as his mate.

Anyway, after a couple of hours of listening to the most inane questions about tour 6A (and attempting to answer without showing too much sarcasm), I realized that I was simply an object for which the four alpha females were jockeying for control. I had another 30 souls flying into Fairbanks to meet me and I couldn't allow this tribe to be my focus of dominance. I solved the problem when someone asked me for the tenth time when they should eat breakfast the following morning.

I looked at the four alpha females (who ranged from age from

36 to 44) and said, "You know, I think I'm going to have a lot of fun with this group this week. We are all about the same age." It was as if I had hit them with a baseball bat. They quickly walked away. Of course, I had alienated them and for the rest of the week had to endure scrutiny not only from the alpha females, but also from the sub-dominant males. One of those males walked with a self important strut and always had a sweater tied around his neck, so I called him Weaselly Little Sweater Boy.

I made sure that all of the activities came off without a hitch, and I was noticing a growing anger amongst the alpha females going into our final day together that they had not been able to exert any dominance over me. It was on this day that they were able to solve this dilemma.

When we arrived in Talkeetna, it was the responsibility of the 46 guests under my stead to advance to the Caribou Room and check in early to their ship. This action would alleviate any long line at the dock in Seward the following day. The tribe had assigned this task to Bleach Blond Monkey Face. For some reason, unknown to me, they thought that they didn't have to be present to check in. Needless to say, when BBMF sat down with her 16 passports and was denied pre boarding privileges by our female representative, Jo Ann, she exploded, "My tour director didn't tell us we had to be present to check in!"

She then noticed that the other representative was a young good looking male, Nick, so she giggled and stuck out her already sagging breasts to make a feminine appeal to him. It didn't work and she stormed out.

When she found me, there was froth extending from both sides of her mouth. She yelled and got close enough to my face that I could see that she had the good starting of a quality mustache, if she would give it a chance. When she had completed her insults, I simply said in a soft voice. "Thank you so much for this advice.

Recommendations like yours will make me a better tour director." I then gave her the same smile she had given me shortly before I had suggested that she was my age three days earlier.

She stomped away.

I was not unhappy to see the tribe leave me at the dock the next day, but as I look over my notes, I do have some observations.

#1 Without exception, the people who give the tour directors the most problems are the East Coast contingents and generally they are led by alpha females: from this, one might gather that a certain degree of tribalism and social inbreeding is taking place on the East Coast. Midwest contingents generally understand manners and politeness, as do West Coasters.

#2 Female dominance creates fear; the other 28 guests seemed to back away from the East Coast tribe. This I lamented the most because there were many quite interesting guests—a 71 year old poet from Las Vegas who has promised to send me his book of poems at no charge, a delightful couple from the Bahamas, a family of four from Pennsylvania, who complimented me every day. Getting along and learning from other people makes this a wonderful job.

#3 Some humans feel that they deserve *special* treatment. They are wrong!

Family Tithes

An aspect of tour directing that generally remains unstated as we meet each new set of three or four dozen guests weekly is *family*. Not the *family* nature that we try to build in order to have a successful tour, but the families from which these guests are originating.

I've noticed that two or three times each touring season, I'll get a group of eight to 12 people who represent one family in different manners and without exception, there will be a matriarch or patriarch (this week it was Wayne from San Diego) who is footing the bill to bring family members together for their 'cruise/tour of a lifetime.' Wayne told me early on that he was paying more than 40,000 dollars for his entourage of nine.

In these family units there is generally a grandfather or grandmother, two or three of their offspring and the associated wives, husbands, and grandchildren. As tour directors, we, like the anthropologist Jane Goodall, observe interactions of the siblings on different levels—who shows dominance —or in most cases who ignores the most—we see them pick theoretical lice from each other's fur by bringing up past painful memories from their usually dysfunctional pasts.

Without exception, these family groups *do not* seem to have a good time and it is *important* for tour directors to *be on top of their game*—because if you mess up in any regard, the entire family of these misfits will have something for which to focus and bond together. In other words—they will turn on you!

I won't make any generalized statements about the family units in our world. I'm sure there are some wonderful *John Boy* type families out there who suck on each other's hypothetical teats for pleasure and spout how wonderful life is; but ,they evidently most often choose not to come on cruise/tours of Alaska.

Here's a few more details about Wayne from San Diego. Wayne paid to have one of his sons go ATV riding with him in Denali National Park—the other son was pissed. The Black Diamond ATV Adventure van had not shown up at the Grande Denali Lodge yet, so I phoned the Bulgarian worker (most of the workers in the park this season are from Bulgaria) who had evidently forgotten, "I be there in ten minutes!"

Right , I thought, *it would be at least 15 minutes*—so, I went out to tell my six waiting ATVers that it would be "a bit longer."

Wayne, who was standing a good distance from the *chosen* son, pulled me aside to talk with me. "You know Fred, I just can't get my kids to like each other. I thought this trip might help, but have you noticed how they ignore each other?"

I nodded yes' thinking that I had also noticed how *all* of them were ignoring him.

"But, I have a surprise for them on the cruise ship, Saturday night. I have made reservations for all the adults at one of those specialty restaurants," he then giggled to himself. "You see Fred, I am dying. Oh, the doctors say that I have a few months left, but no one in my family knows anything about this. I have accumulated a lot of money and other stuff in my life and I am going to tell everyone that unless they start showing more love for each other, they will get none of it. My lawyers have everything drawn up pretty tight."

Wayne then went on to tell me about some of the vastness of his material empire and fortunately for me the Bulgarian driver arrived and whisked the ATVers away.

I shook my head as I watched the white van disappear and wrote down one more statement in my mental Jane Goodall notebook. Wayne is a man who simply doesn't get it!

We're All Family

Roberta and I were proud of ourselves as we awaited at Pike's Hotel for our 5:11 PM arrivals from the Fairbanks Airport. We had found two Mosher's on her manifest who were flying in on the same plane as the eight Mosher's I had on my manifest. Mosher was not a common name, or so we thought, so, we had switched some people around so that all of the Mosher's could be together in my group.

As it turned out, these two separate namesakes did not know each other—and their differences in familiarity were a minor aspect in relation to their natures.

Some of the most humorous episodes of the Andy Griffith Show of the 1960s (The most popular TV show for many years.) involved the Darlings. When these hill people came into Mayberry, a fictitious North Carolina town, Sheriff, Andy Taylor, and Deputy, Barney Fife, would be kept busy managing to temper the clash of lifestyles of the modern people of Mayberry and the *basic* nature of the Darlings. The directors of this sitcom were careful not to portray these hill people as lesser humans by having them play and sing country music.

"Don't play that song Pa. It makes me cry," Charlene would say, even to the point of creating a troublemaker amongst them, Ernest T. Bass.

Anyway, I bring this up because occasionally we get divergent groups on our tours and must develop strategies so that they can live together peacefully for four, five, or six days.

The two Mosher families had that divergence.

The original eight Moshers that were on my manifest were from Oklahoma City and most definitely represented the Darlings. The second Moshers were from Dallas, Texas and were traveling with another couple, the Bobergs—a 1960s television reference which might work for these people's nature would be Mr. and Mrs. Thurston Howell III from the *Gilligan's Island* series. All four wore sweaters tied in a knot over their shoulders and the men wore the spit shine loafers which had the sash on top.

In my introductions, I made no mention to the Oklahoma Moshers of the other Texas Moshers, but later in the week, when a bag was misplaced into Kevin Mosher's room Kevin had said to me, "Fred, we gotta meet these other Mosher's. We might be kin" (Kevin, the most animated of the Oklahoma Moshers, had stood up the first day on the motor coach when he realized that one of the items to find on my Sightseeing Bingo game was a man missing a tooth, and yelled to everyone "Ya all can check off this," he smiled—showing that he had no upper teeth at all, "I got's no teeth at all.")

I agreed, but based upon the way the wealthy Mosher's had been avoiding Kevin and his clan I chose not to initiate anything—until one of the Mrs. Thurston Howell III came up to me a day later and said in a rather snooty manner. "You know something, Fred! The last name Mosher is a very common name. You shouldn't have moved us from Roberta's group."

"I haven't met many Mosher's." I responded, trying to act as nasally elegant as she, "I guess that Roberta and I messed up. Sorry."

It was when our tour #1 was leaving Denali Park on the motor coach to begin a 240 mile trek down to Anchorage that I inadvertently got my Moshers together. Because of there being many groups and a large number (53 seats taken out of 56) of guests—I had to load groups front to back two separate times—so that all people had a chance to sit toward the front.

"I need the Moshers to load now!" I announced and I noticed one of the Mr. Thurston Howell III hustling over to me. "You don't mean *all* of the Mosher's do you?" he whispered.

"Yes, all of the Moshers." I said, so that Kevin could hear and who immediately ran to me. "Hi Mr. Mosher. I'm Mr. Mosher!" Kevin smiled showing off his gums and putting his arm around the nervous looking Mr. Mosher. "We're gunna get to know you. We're all family!"

I smiled.

Testing Limits

I stood in the parking lot of the Grande Denali Lodge holding 24 room key packets in my hands, while awaiting the Tundra Wilderness Tour bus #24 to make its final few switchbacks up the 300 foot hill to its destination. Aboard this metal chariot (converted school bus) were my 51 guests on Tour #6. I felt reasonably confident. I had checked their rooms and had found five misplaced bags, supplied the family of seven with a comfortable car seat for their one year old child, and the weather was remarkable.

But, this was one of four or five of tours that test the limits of our guests. We ask the guests to put their bags out in their hotel's hallway at 6 AM. Then, to board our motor coach and proceed to the train depot, where they will spend the next four and a half hours viewing amazing scenery, while enjoying a delicious breakfast. If this were the major extent of the guest's day, then I wouldn't be writing this story. But, we then have them grab a quick lunch at the Visitor's Center in Denali National Park and jump on a park bus that holds 52 people. Oh, did I also mention that I have three gentlemen who weigh more than 350 pounds?

This bus takes them 55 miles, no, 63 miles, since its a clear day, into the park where they then turn around and return the 63 miles on a bumpy, gravel road.

I can now see the bus approaching and some of the painful looks on their once joyful faces, from eight hours earlier. Did I mention that it is now 10 PM?

No matter how entertaining and educational the bus driver was, how beautiful the Alaska scenery had impressed, or how many wild animals had been seen—the fact of being cramped up on a school bus for this amount of time—with only four short bathroom breaks precludes most jovial interaction with their tour director upon arrival—did I mention that I have played this key holding anticipatory role around five dozen times?

I could hear the screaming child as the bus rolled to a stop. There was a pall over the guests faces as they dragged themselves to me to get their room keys—this meant that they had seen few animals. So, my role would be to quickly get them to their rooms and try to explain their eating options at the hotel this late at night—another totally limit testing opportunity.

The 65 year old Mr. Coburn re-approached me after I had given him his keys and he had read Check Out Time at 10 AM. "Fred! I am going on an ATV trip tomorrow morning. I have to have a shower after I get back, and you're telling me I have to be out of my room?" he yelled, a few inches from my face.

I hadn't been yelled at for a few years, so I was a bit taken back, but, was thinking that I was very glad I had found one of his misplaced bags and put it into the proper room. A double mistake really makes people snap. "Well, yes. Sir, you might request a later time at the front desk. This is the hotel's policies, not mine." I tried to sound calm as many of my other guests watched.

He angrily marched away and I finished handing out the keys.

I then waited in the lobby another 20 minutes for any other issues that might crop up and cringed as Mr. Coburn walked up. I had seen him drinking wine with his wife and the two other couples, he was traveling with.

"I got the front desk to let me stay in our room longer. I am sorry that I yelled at you. I am going through Chemo right now and pushed this trip, Cindy and I have been planning for our whole lives, between treatments." he said, while his hands shook uncontrollably. He then hugged me and whispered in my ear, "That bus ride was too damn long".

Osama Meets Boss Hog

This tour was the most difficult of the 30 or so tours I directed in 2001 and 2002. Really, it was only difficult in perception. What I do is help 35 or so people each week through a pre-designed script on one of the 13 land tours that our company offers in Alaska. The people have signed up for their specific tour and usually have some concept of what is in store for them. I simply try my best to make sure everything happens as it should.

And to be perfectly honest, it was a difficult tour because of my own personal perceptions. I guess I should start from the beginning. This particular tour #12 was what is called a turn-around. I had a group (tour #13) already at Alyeska Hotel, which I was going to take to the ship in Seward (90 miles south) around 2 PM, but in the meantime I had to get up at 7 AM and drive down and pick up the 35 people (tour #12) who had just arrived on the ship. I then brought them up to the Alyeska Hotel, only to turn around and head back to Seward with my original group.

This job is all about first impressions. The people's first impression of me and mine of them. When a tour director is asked to manage two groups simultaneously; well, sometimes, it simply doesn't work so well.

To add to this chemistry, I was traveling with two other motor coaches whose tour directors were Deb and Joy; both of whom I had truly enjoyed being with the previous week. Deb is my age and is as spontaneously funny and witty as any woman I've ever met. Joy is a 32-year-old, tall, blonde haired beauty who's quiet, sexy nature is furthered in distraction to the male by the fact that she has a twin sister named Karma, who matches her in every way. I assure you that a story exists on my interactions with these two ladies, but it will take some more processing on my part to understand how the three of us worked those two weeks.

So, I have excuses for not being at the top of my game. I believe that the only excuse I really can use is that in my lifetime I have never understood prejudice. Oh, I know what it is, have witnessed it in various ways throughout my life, but to crawl into its secure niche and explore its machinations, to understand why people allow it to disgrace their words and actions, is a bit out of my realm of thought.

On this tour #12, I had a family of nine from India and New Jersey and I had a group of six couples from Dallas, Texas who were traveling together. The group from India belonged to a religious sect that required the men to have cloth wrapped upon their heads. The gentleman whom arranged the trip was a dentist from New Jersey and his wife had always wanted to see Alaska. They also had three children and they had, in addition, flown his mother and three other relatives from New Delhi, India. One of the relatives was a rather ominous looking, tall, dark-skinned young man who rarely smiled.

I knew that this chemistry might be tough, so I went out of my way to be as friendly as I could with the Al Qaeda, as I overheard the Texans call them. Also, the tall unfriendly looking Indian was nicknamed, Osama.

So, to Joy and Deb, my group was Al Qaeda vs. Dukes of Hazard, but Joy and Deb didn't know about another couple who added a special flavoring to the situation I am about to tell you about. Their names were Ned and Judy from Minnesota. They were traveling alone. Ned was a retired Lutheran minister and Judy sold Amway.

The first morning I did my count. All tour directors have to count their passengers before they leave any location. "Twenty-five, twenty-six. Looks like we're missing nine people." I pulled out the list of names and began to read off the list. "Fred," Boss Hog, the largest and obvious leader of the Dallas contingent, interrupted, "I think its the ragheads."

I gave him something of a sneer and ran into the lobby to call some rooms —but as always happens when I get all the numbers pushed, the elevator opens and there they are—at least five of them, anyway. It took approximately five to ten minutes to get the entire family rounded up and onto the motor coach. The looks of disgust were apparent on most of the rest of the group.

I sighed.

Many of the tour directors and some drivers make a point of trying to subtly threaten the passengers to be on time, telling them that if they are late twice, they may just see only the back of the motor coach as it pulls away. I find this tacky. In my two seasons, I had never had anyone be more than 10 minutes late and the idea of publicly embarrassing anyone because they were a few minutes late, for me anyway, was not acceptable. These people had paid a high price for this trip and I had no right to be a negative remembrance—besides it could hurt tips.

We drove the group to Anchorage, spotting several Dall sheep on the cliffs around Turnagain Arm along the way. We then dropped them off downtown at the Saturday Market. Here, we allowed them two and a half hours to have lunch and shop around Alaska's largest city. It was one of those truly beautiful sunny days, so I was assured a good time would be had by all.

When they returned, once again I counted to 26 and stopped. I could hear the Texans grumbling again and we spotted the Indians sauntering toward us a few blocks away.

"I really appreciate everyone's patience concerning our foreign passengers," I said trying to stem off a mutiny. "I have had many similar occurrences in the past. Getting used to customs in new countries can be difficult."

We arrived two and a half hours later at Talkeetna. We would be spending two evenings here before boarding the train that would take us up to Denali National Park. It was my hope that the group would mix more during this day and a half and we wouldn't have the anger I had seen already, but just to make sure before they disembarked to their hotel rooms I announced:

"Be sure to try and be on time when we leave for the trains. I've been told that trains wait for nobody," I laughed trying not to point fingers and I caught some of my Texans winking at me.

During our time in Talkeetna, I noticed that both the Dukes and the Al Qaeda had wisely used the great weather to fly to view Mt. McKinley up close. This always put the passengers in an awe stuck manner and all problems generally end.

The next morning I was feeling reasonably confident that everyone would load onto the motor coach and we would make a quick trip to the train depot to board our northbound train. That confidence was short-lived as I glanced through the motor coach and saw empty seats that had been filled the previous two days. Tourists rarely move from the seats they first sit in. I sighed and Boss Hog noticed it.

"Now Fred," he began with a slur of sorts. I suddenly remembered that the six Dallas couples were making their way into the bar, as I was leaving after having my molehill cheesecake and whiskey and water. "We've been patient. Now these Ragheads are going to make us miss our train!"

"Calm down sir." I almost said Boss. "I'm sure they will be here in just a minute," I said and decided to wait outside the motor coach, where if it got really ugly I wouldn't have to bear the brunt of it.

I was surprised to see Osama standing right by the door leading into the motor coach. I smiled nervously and asked him if his family would be coming soon. He gave me an angry look and shrugged his shoulders.

Suddenly there came a chant from inside the motor coach; Leave the Ragheads. Leave the Ragheads. Leave the Ragheads. Leave the Ragheads."

I giggled. I always giggle when I'm frightened. Then heard Ned the Minnesota preacher interrupt them. "Let's stop this chanting. This is not being Christian."

Osama quickly jumped onto the motor coach and I followed. "Even though our non Christian friends have been keeping us waiting...." Osama had a flare for the dramatic and stood only a few inches behind Ned, towering over him with an intense look of anger on his face. I was able to glance over Osama's shoulder and see the truly frightened looks on everyone's face.

"The Bible tells us...." Ned said in his most theatric manner. Then, he noticed his wife pointing behind him. He turned around to see Osama's menacing stare.

"Holy ...," Ned managed and quickly took his seat.

"What is this all about?" Osama yelled in a tone that even made my hair curl a little.

I let four or five seconds pass by and scanned the Texans with their red faces, reflecting the cowardice that travels with ignorant prejudice. "We were just being silly," I assured him and noticed his eight family members boarding. "Looks like we're all here. Let's head to the depot."

Our motor coach driver, Fred, took a deep sigh and we took off. That moment seemed to solidify the group. I did some major mingling on the train with all the passengers to help the process along.

When the Texans found out that Osama's uncle was a very wealthy dentist from New Jersey, they warmed up to the whole entourage. Both groups had similar expensive digital camera equipment, so there was a common bond.

Even on the last day, when Osama's Aunt accidently dropped her diamond ring between the wooden slats at the Alaska Oil Pipeline turnout in Fairbanks, everyone got on their hands and knees to try and recover it. When it was finally found everybody cheered.

So, I guess that this tour ended up being enjoyable for all. But, there was a moment when I was about ready to turn in my smile.

Buy and Sell

"Do you buy into this or that idea?" We hear that phrase often, but what does it mean? It means, from my way of thinking, that we, in this society, are viewed by the powers that be as economic entities. This use of economic terminology drifts into all of our worlds. We buy into political, religious, and social affiliations, and we sell our services for what we are told to be just causes.

So, how does this random idea fit into my world of tour directing? It fits because most of the guests on tour #6 this week were super excited to be driving through the Wasilla that is the hometown of possibly our country's next vice president. They ignored the majestic Chugach Mountains in the background and their first view of the Pacific Ocean, Knik Arm, off to their right. They, as millions of others around this country, have bought into the importance of this political reality.

I yawned.

It seemed that the guests, who were in the age group above the mid-60s, weren't all that interested. They realized how extraordinary the scenery was and seeing all of Alaska's infinite beauty and knowing that political notoriety is most often fleeting at best.

But why has our society become the way it has?

My driver this week was a fine young man named Daniel, who was driving one of his final tours after three years of service to our company. He told me that he had just completed the school work required to become an air traffic controller and would seek employment at an airport in the western US after our season ends next week.

"I had a good job in masonry for a few years, but it was back-breaking work and I saw how many accidents occurred in this profession and how quickly people aged." Daniel then showed me some of his scars from that work. "While in high school, our class got to visit an air traffic control tower. That's how I got the bug. It will be better for me to use my mind to make a living rather than my muscle."

I had a similar experience when I was 20 and working as a laborer in Eugene, Oregon. I decided to return to college and seek a less physically demanding career—which led to my teaching career.

Physically exerting jobs used to be called 'an honest day's work' a few generations back. Does that imply that other jobs can be less than honest? Did I see dishonesty in the teaching field? Yes. The nature of some jobs, themselves, may be dishonest. The enticement to slack off also exists and is often taken. Did I see slovenly educators? Yes. Many. But, I must also admit that I also saw dedicated, hard working teachers who became incredible influences in young people's lives.

Sarah Palin was asked recently if she was going to relinquish her position as governor of Alaska, now that she would be campaigning daily nationwide until the election in November?

"Oh no," she replied with her winning smile, "I'll still be the governor of our great state.

This pleads the question; what does the governor of a state really do? What do people who reach high up on their corporate ladders or political positions really do? How are they accountable for 'an honest day's work'?

I will allow these notions to pass—as they must—and concentrate on the 80-year-old man, Mr. Shafer, who shook my right hand with both of his hands yesterday on Fourth Avenue in Anchorage and said, "My wife and I have saved for this vacation all of our lives. I want to thank you for making it such a wonderful experience. I'll be emailing you to tell you about our cruise!"

What I am buying into as a tour director are these special moments of kindness that people, whom you have just met, convey to you for a job well done.

There are some gifts that can never be sold.

A Curious Lot

Tour directors are a curious lot. There can be absolutely no denying this statement. In my nine summers of being a tour director I have met probably around seven or eight score of individuals who have worn this label (the photo contains four of some of our most unique ones). In order to be a successful tour director there are some basic specifics that must reside within your character in some manner.

Four truly unique tour directors.

- Patience: when the guest shows up late each morning to load the motor coach the TD must decide a reaction that is a balance from wringing their necks, talking tersely to them, or ignoring it (I always choose the latter).
- Kindness: There are guests whom simply are unable to work well in group settings (which our full tours especially are) either physically or psychologically. Tour directors must find kindness within themselves to adapt accordingly. As an example, Sharon, my wheelchair lady this week, asked me to lean down

and lift her foot onto the four inch rise on the train car. I leaned down to lift it and it twisted oddly and I realized it wasn't a real foot; an awkward moment that nearly made me scream.

• Humor: We have joke tellers and non-joke tellers. The guests usually love the jokes. I just can't tell them. For example, when the driver explains the bumpy ice heaved highway north of Denali Park they generally say, "It's not my fault. It's not Fred's fault. It's the asphalt ... ha ha ha." This is wordplay, which I love, but can't do it—too predictable.

• Discretion: Tour directors might find it in their best interest to keep their personal opinions about politics, religion, and other sundry topics that might offend to themselves. As an example, this week I had two preachers and their wives from Arkansas on tour with me. They were very nice couples, who yelled out "praise be to God" for no apparent reason while we all rode the motor coach. When one of them asked me, "How can one not believe in Jesus Christ as our lord and savior when viewing this incredible scenery?" All I could say was, "Yes, sometimes people cannot help but cry on beautiful days like this."

• Valor: Kind of an odd word and I never would have included it as a tour director trait before this past week. But I definitely showed valor to one of my guests, Carlos Rivera. As I walked onto Alaska Airlines flight #182, which would fly my tour #12A group from Fairbanks to Anchorage, I glanced to my left and saw Carlos, a slim, mid-50s man who was traveling with his wife, Maria, and ten year old daughter, Sophia, sitting in the bulkhead row between two men whom each had to weigh in excess of 350 pounds. I snickered to myself at the suffering he would have to endure and then found an empty seat beside myself in row 24, which was just behind his wife and daughter. Alaska Airlines oftentimes separates our guests on full flights. I quickly made my way forward and helped pry Carlos from between the two behemoths.

•No Word Available in the English Language: When you have the guest that feels that he or she must ask you a question every time they see you, and the question has to somehow stump you. I had Herman Jinstill from Maryland who asked me question after question—and much to his chagrin each time I had a decent answer—until we were waiting to walk out to the motor coach at the airport in Anchorage. "Fred. You said that Mt. McKinley was growing about a centimeter a year and in a million years I figured that it will be more than 50,000 feet high. Won't that throw the rotation of the earth out of kilter?"

I shook my head and said, "You got me on that one Herman." He smiled and walked out of my life.

Riley Creek Bridge
Occasionally moments in our lives give us a
firm, little shake This was one of those moments.

The north bound Alaska Railroad passenger train moved slowly
over the nearly 100-foot-high Riley Creek bridge (built in 1922).
It always gave the passengers a thrill to look down and view
the clear runoff waters of Riley Creek mixing with a glacial wa-
ter creek, nearly directly  under the bridge—it was
new water mixing with very
old water. Today, several of
the guests on the second
white train car, that held a
large, painted grizzly bear
on the exterior, spotted
something in the distance that seemed a bit odd. They saw what
looked to be a tall, young man, and a nearly as tall young woman
standing a foot deep in the undoubtably very cold waters of Riley Creek. None of the train-goers who had spotted these two
people (whom also seemed to have their heads bowed) made any
comment, as they further viewed them through their binoculars.
These guests to this northern world were too excited about their
momentary arrival into Denali National Park. Alaska was such a
foreign place, mentally, to the 160 or so guests whom occupied

these two train cars, that whatever the motive could have been for these two young people standing in the cold, creek water, they easily accepted that it was probably something beyond their present spectrum of understanding.

But, nearly three miles away, in the lobby of the hotel of which these two young people were staying—I knew. These two young people had taken a 6:30 AM Tundra Wilderness Tour into the park with their two aunts and an uncle. These three older people were now very animated as they told me of the wonderful time they had had viewing not only four large mammals: moose, caribou, grizzly bears, and dall sheep, that inhabit the park, but also they showed me digital photos of a fox, a lynx, and a, base to peak, view of Mount McKinley.

Yeah, I thought to myself, *these good folks had hit the tourist jackpot for sightseeing in this national park!'*

But, I noticed that the two young people were not with them. I was hesitant to bring up their absence, since the day before, I had made the error of thinking that this brother and sister were a young married couple, when they complained about having a king sized bed at our hotel in Denali. To be fair to myself, I hadn't met them at the meet and greet, since their Delta Airlines flight didn't arrive in Fairbanks until the next morning.

"Fred. We are brother and sister!" they had yelled with a laugh, and I felt my face turn red—I quickly switched them to a room with two beds.

"So, where's the kids?" I asked the three older ones, as I finished looking at their camera's photos.

"Oh, they hiked down that Riley Creek trail we were on yesterday." I had accompanied a group of 23 guests on the three hour Discover Denali Tour.

I then gave the man a curious look, since it certainly seemed odd that anyone would want to go on a three mile hike after riding on a school bus for eight hours, no matter what their age. The older man then pulled me aside.

"Fred, I'm sorry that we didn't get to talk because of our late flight into Fairbanks. The kids lost their father to prostrate cancer only four weeks before the three of them were to come on this trip up here to Alaska. Their father had saved money for this vacation for a long time and even has had a lifelong subscription to *Alaska* magazine. I have no idea why he never came up here before. He would have loved it!! Anyway, the kids brought a very small canister of his ashes along... and both of them agreed that the Riley Creek Trail was so beautiful, that that spot down near the train trestle was where they knew he would love to be."

I shook my head and thanked him for sharing this with me.

But, it was 20 minutes later, when I was relating this story to my wife, Celia, that, as I said the words 'spreading his ashes,' I felt tears welling up in my eyes, and I could not continue the conversation. It seems that we, whom live in this beautiful, north country, must never allow the beauty we witness, and show off to visitors, to be taken for granted. As I awaited the wave of emotion to pass within me, I realized that I had not taken it for granted—it had taken me to someplace much more special.

Breaking In Ops

Working in the *ops* department of our company can be a hectic reality... with 21 different Alaska land tour patterns involving 52 motor coaches, four train cars, nearly 300 employees, and of course our estimated 32,000 guests, one can only imagine the types of situations that can, and do occur.

This season we once again have some new employees working in ops and one employee, Meagan, an extremely kind and sweet 20 year old who worked at the Marriott as a greeter last season, had the misfortune to answer the phone when I called to her department a couple of days ago.

"Hello, this is Meagan in ops. How may I help you?" Meagan sweetly answered.

"Hi Meagan, this is Fred on tour 20A in Denali Park, at the Village, and I have a problem."

"What is it Fred?"

"A guest left an item in her room at Pike's up in Fairbanks, and it is very important to her—and for some odd reason, the phone numbers I have won't connect me to that hotel."

"Okay, Fred. What is the item?"

"A colorful silk sarong," I replied. The woman described it as a colorful house coat, but for my motives—it would be a sarong.

"What is that?" Meagan asked with a laugh.

"It's some kind of woman's garment that you wrap around. A friend gave it to her as a pre wedding gift. She's getting married on the ship, when they get to it. And, oh yeah, she said it was long."

"So, you are missing a long, sarong?" Meagan laughed.

"Yes," I replied, getting into the conversation, "Is anything wrong?"

"What is the guest's name?"

"Miss Wong... soon to be Mrs., I guess,"

"I need her whole name Fred," Meagan replied now sounding a bit peeved.

"Are you sure that you need this Meagan?"

"Yes, Fred on tour 20A... the form has a spot for a first and middle name!"

"Okay, her entire name is Mary Wing Wah Wong and she's from Hong Kong."

"Are you messing with me, Fred... I was warned about you and your humor."

"Why would I be messing with you Meagan? You always are so happy. Now, repeat what I have told you so far."

"Miss Mary Wing Wah Wong from Hong Kong has lost her long, sarong. Fred, I don't think that name exists!!"

"Look on my manifest. Fifth name down," I replied and added, "Will this take long?"

Thirty seconds or so later. "I see your guest's name and I will call the hotel to see where the sarong might belong. Anything else Fred?" Meagan said, obviously proud of her rhyming comeback.

"Just that this sarong was very expensive. But, her friend said that she was able to get it for 'a song.'"

I heard the phone click on the other end. I didn't get a chance to say 'so long.'

The Power of Thought and Float Trips in Talkeetna

Ralph Waldo Emerson... in his essay on 'Fate' wrote; "Nothing befalls us, that we do not invite."

These eight words track a deep trowel into the earth of my thinking these day. I will state my reasoning.

I lost a touring friend this summer who *invited* illness into his being when he turned 60 years of age. He had never struck me as a hypochondriac before and I wondered his motives when he hit the three score mark in years and began to complain about every possible ailment that he thought might be affecting him. He pursued doctor after doctor whom, each, found nothing significantly wrong with him, but catered to his insecurities by providing him with punishing medicines and procedures, which, in my opinion, did, two years later, put his name into the obituary column. This ill-begotten thought concerning his mortality, did him in.

Thus, I will add my eight words to complete Emerson's notion of a century and a half ago; "Simultaneously, we are and become what we think."

This job of Celia and mine of tour directing in Alaska provides a well equipped laboratory to pursue this hypothesis... with our smiles, our candies, our calming and entertaining commentary, and of course our magical birch burls, we track eternal this notion of our all powerful thoughts.

With these words, may I introduce you to Rose and Bernie?

Each of these individuals had no idea that they would be sharing space on my tour #12 this week, but the power of a thought fashioned a coincidence that still has me scratching my head as I write these words.

Rose and her husband, from Long Island, New York, had wanted to bring their entire family on a trip to Alaska a few years earlier, but two of their grandchildren were too young to travel, so they put off the trip. Unfortunately, shortly after this idea was hatched, Rose's husband suddenly passed away—but Rose would not allow the idea of this trip to die.

I, of course, knew nothing of this as I met the New York family of six adults and six children in the lobby of the Marriott hotel in Anchorage last Sunday. "Before you all head to your rooms, I see that you have all booked the Talkeetna River Float for tomorrow at 2:30 PM," I said and they all concurred that they had done this as a whim on their computer several weeks earlier.

"And are the W…s also with your group?" I asked since there was another couple signed up for the same excursion, at the same time.

"No," Rose said with a twinkle in her eyes, "But that name certainly sounds familiar."

I didn't think too much more about this until the next day, when Bernie W approached me and asked if he and his wife could cancel the float trip, since Talkeetna was experiencing a fairly steady rainfall. I made a phone call to our office and was able to release them from this obligation and then asked him if he knew whether or not the family of 12 also wanted to cancel their trip?

"They still want to go," Bernie responded, "And do you want to hear something strange?"

I nodded my head and smiled, hoping for something interesting.

"Rose and her husband were good friends of mine, more than 30 years ago. He and I worked together in a computer company we both were developing. I heard of his passing a few years ago and have always lamented not driving the few hundred miles, so I could attend his funeral. Isn't it odd that we would meet here?"

I agreed with him that it was indeed quite a coincidence, especially since this excursion was one of the less booked of our pre-books, and that they had signed up for it at the same time. There were three separate times they could have signed up.

The next day on the train, as we were traveling to Denali National Park, I told Rose that I had spoken with Bernie (who was sitting with his wife around 10 rows in front of the Long Island group) concerning the coincidence. The mid-seventies Rose held my hand and began;

"Bernie was a great friend of ours three decades ago as my husband and I were starting the business. In fact, I think that he was a huge part of the success we eventually attained. Also, I have a photo collage Bernie made of a 4th of July picnic we had for the company, so many years ago. He got married and moved many miles away and we simply lost track of each other."

I thought that our conversation was over, then Rose got closer to me. "I went into a darkened room at our home before we came on this trip and told my husband, that if I was going to still finance this huge family trip up north, that he was going to have to, in some way, show us that he was still with us in spirit."

She hesitated, as some guests passed us, on their way downstairs to lunch. "I found a penny at the airport in Anchorage that was dated 1960—the year we were married—and I thought that that was the *sign*. But, now I see that he brought Bernie back into our lives. I am sure that my husband is here, Fred."

The goose bumps were securely attached to my arms, as I sighed and made my way back to my tour director nook, at the back of the train car.

Hear Our Song

Back in April, as Celia and I psychologically prepared for this tour directing season, I recall hearing a sound from nature which reminded me of a calling that our consciousness continually gives to all of us; loneliness. I was reading an Emerson book, as the sun began to lighten the early Spring Alaskan skies, when the sound began. I set the book down for a bit and registered three distinct songs originating from a lone male robin, whom was seeking a mate.

Our northern winter's distance in time is only matched by an equally elongated expression of silence—that this lonely robin broke, along with the chatter of a tree squirrel. These sounds ended winter's hold—releasing thoughts for warmer more active times.

Why does this auditory image bring these words to paper on this rainy September morning?

My final group of 32 guests are a needy bunch. At least half a dozen of them are chirping inane questions, spouting tedious life stories, or worrying constantly about each nuance of the weather. They chirp, not for a mate, but for recognition.

This group dynamic is not at all unique to any of the scores of groups we have led through Alaska, but the sound that I now hear outside of our window is not the robin calling, but instead, the honking of our yearly nesting pair of sandhill cranes. Having successfully raised two young, the four majestic birds are flying up to join a larger array of cranes in the higher altitudes, whom are forming large Vs in preparation for heading south.

Evidently, there is not a season for loneliness.

I do hope that some of the 16 couples on my final tour of this season, all traveling alone, will somehow make friends with each other—but based upon the silence thus far on the motor coach and the overzealous laughter at my meager attempts at humor, I have my doubts. If, indeed, I am belittling these late season tourists, then I must also admit to belittling myself; since I am—we all are of the same tribe. We all call for someone to relieve the pain of our personal loneliness. We are alone. We all know it and sense that this state of being is not one with which we care to embrace.

My four squared couples have invested in this 12-day northern adventure in many ways and will surely enjoy Alaska. They have already seen Mount McKinley clearly from the base to the peak. But, they are beginning to realize that if somehow they can establish new friendships before they board their luxurious cruise ship, that their time at sea will most assuredly be enriched.

We all call to each other.

We all want to be recognized.

Hear our song.

Postscript

I wrote the above words on day two of a six day tour and now that the final cruise tour of the season is complete…I am pleased to report that 15 of the 16 couples matched up well with some other couple on our tour. The sixteenth couple might have fared better had our company sponsored this last tour as an *Aliens Amongst Us* tour.

The following stories are from adventures from aboard cruise ships. As workers for our company, we are allowed reduced priced passage on cruise ships.

Wordplay in the Caribbean

Jack, formerly known as TD #1, led the six of us around a few blocks to a bus station where, for $5 round trip, we could go to Hell and back. Yes, there was a small community on Grand Cayman Island, 9 miles from downtown Georgetown, named Hell.

Once there, we were dropped off at a gift shop that resided in front of a very strange rock outcropping that with a little imagi-nation looked like the fires of Hell—or as anyone ever considered them to be. The gift shop sold shot glasses, tee shirts, magnets, and any other touristy items one could think of, all emblazoned with Bought in Hell. The most creative item was a hand basket; i.e. go to Hell in

Jack and Jenn oddly looking natural.

a hand basket. Celia wouldn't buy it, "I'm not paying $15 for a damn hand basket!" she said. Obviously, she knew the going rate for hand baskets better than I did.

The most peculiar reality of Hell was an odd, little man who walked around in a devil's outfit with red horns. He met everyone with a handshake and a "How in the Hell are you?" He also had a wooden cutout of himself in front of the Hell Gift Shop, where photos could be taken. He would kiss all of the women he saw and announce loudly, with a little bit of a Spanish accent., "You have now been kissed by the Devil." He would then laugh and offer to show them his upper arm tattoo, which when looked at one way was appropriate, but when looked at another way was extremely inappropriate.

The devil was a kind of a slimy, little guy, but I ventured to guess that he

The Monica and Darcy welcoming party.

had pretty good job security. I mean, how could the Devil screw up? He convinced one of the girls to kiss him and then turned his head as she tried to kiss his cheek.

We were stuck in Hell for about 20 minutes too long, as our bus didn't return. Finally the Devil came and told us to go wait out along the road. We had been huddled in the shade in his parking lot. It was hotter than Hell in Hell. We walked a hundred yards, or so, along the road and got a photo of a road sign that was marked HELL—we were on the road to Hell.

Monica and Jack hanging in Hell.

The bus finally pulled up and the driver asked, "Why are you waiting out here in the heat?"

We told him that the Devil told us to come here to wait.

"Never listen to him. What in Hell does the Devil know?"

153

Simple Truths #1 and #2

Occasionally, in this wonderful life into which each of us has been placed, days occur that define possibilities of perception. Yesterday was one such day. It was a day where Celia and I spent time with four friends—all in search of discovery in a strange land; yet, within these seven hours of unique socialization—marked by much hilarity, some education, and decided moments of surprise, there were whispers (for those attuned to listen) of simple truths.

Truth #1 We are not as secure as we believe ourselves to be.

I was sitting upon a picnic table that was positioned just to the Caribbean Sea side of a sandy trail about a kilometer into a 5K adventure walk. Our Costa Rican guide had dropped us off here and promised to pick us up three hours later. We were informed that by conquering the 5K trail we might see howler monkeys, three toed sloths, a variety of tropical birds, and iguanas. Thus far, I had seen a dime-sized hermit crab making its way across the trail. So, I made a personal decision to stop and rest at this picnic table and mentally review the excitement I had thus far experienced in this outdoor sauna. Celia, Jenn, Darcy, Monica, and Scott (a singer the girls had befriended onboard the ship) went on their way and I promised to follow.

I was just about to get up and continue the suffering when I heard this blood-curdling, deep throated growl emanating from the trail in the direction I *had* intended to pursue. I have never heard a monkey make a sound like this. At that moment, I saw two German couples (our ship is half-filled with German occupants) running toward me from the direction of the terror-filled growl.

"Was ist das?" they yelled at me and for the first time in my life I got to use the four years of German I took in high school. Miss Hewitt, my lesbian German teacher would be so proud.

I shrugged my shoulders and then smiled because one of the men was at least 30 pounds heavier than me and if the animal that had increased my heartbeat by a factor of three came bounding around the curve in the trail, I was pretty certain I could outrun Klaus. I joined their group and made haste to the trailhead.

I later found out that Celia and the young ones had encountered the same growl with only Celia,

Howler Monkey

Monica, and Scott wishing to retreat while Jenn and Darcy chose to photograph whatever it was making the noise.

Three of the five were hearing the whispers from Truth #1 (it turned out to be a howler monkey making the frightening sound).

After the national park trip, the owner of the van joined her driver because a person at the dock had marked our group down as being on a different ship, which left the dock at 2:30 PM, and our ship was to leave at 7 PM. This was a great bonus for us because the owner was articulate in English, besides being a true beauty, and shared much interesting information with us about her country.

After the Howling Monkey Incident (HMI), they took the six of us to two *banana plantations*: one owned by Chiquita and one

owned by Del Monte. A very large Caucasian boss man came out of the office at Chiquita and told us to leave. We saw 50 or so dark-skinned workers washing, placing stickers, and boxing the green bananas. But, before we were kicked out, our driver stole a case of bananas and put them in the back of the van.

At Del Monte's, the workers were gone, their 5 AM to 3 PM shift being over. We found out that most plantations employ

around 150 workers, that it takes one stalk (about 15 feet high) about nine months to produce one bunch of bananas after which the stalk is cut down and a new stalk will grow from the roots, Costa Rica is one of the top four banana exporting countries, bananas are harvested year round, at the bottom of each bunch there is a lone male banana that pointed upward in a rather provocative manner.

"So," I asked the attractive owner of the van, "that one lone banana services the hundred or so female bananas above it?"

"Yes!" she responded, not hesitating, "Notice how small it is.

When it is finished it is *cut off* and thrown away. It is of no further use!

All of the girls laughed and I felt a bit uncomfortable. I then asked if all the workers were well paid.

"No," she responded, "they bring in very poor Nicaraguans— slaves really—who live in those shanties over there." She pointed to some structures which were purposely hidden by the vegetation.

"Can't the government of Costa Rica do something to get better paying jobs for Costa Ricans?"

She rolled her eyes at me, "It's our government who brings in the foreign workers."

I sighed, as I recalled my own heritage. My grandfather Ray lived in a company built house and shopped for groceries at the company owned store. His bill there generally exceeded what his meager salary in the coal mine paid him; making him in Eastern Kentucky in 1947 (the year he died of black lung at age 49) very similar, in condition, to the Nicaraguans farming bananas in 2008 in Costa Rica.

My grandparents and their four children. My dad is the only one smiling.

Truth #2 does state that we simply cannot allow poverty or death to get in the way of good, cheap labor.

Time, Sloths, Interlopers, and Tourists

Time: The thing that we call by this name to explain what has led up to *now* and what *now* means in relation to what might happen next. It tends to help explain our reality in a more rational manner, but I'm reasonably convinced that once time ceases, as we know it, its illusion will be made obvious.

Time and Sloths: Sloths used to be giants a hundred million years ago—but something happened 85 million years which separated them—making them shrink and become armadillos in the north part of Central America and southern part of North America and shrink and also become three and two toed sloths in the south—two extremely odd animals.

We speak of 100 million years in a rather cavalier manner, but if we shrink that period of time into one of our days, then our possible 100 years of life would take up a little less than one second of that day. Then, also consider that since the year 1900, adult males in the (well fed) USA have gone from an average height of 5-foot 6-inches to an average height of 5-foot 11-inches today. At this rate all men will be more than seven feet in height by the year 2300. Adaptation is a dynamic force in this life, which we rarely put into the proper perspective.

Sloths: These South and Central American animals live only

in trees which provide them with all of their food (they even get their water from the leaves). They hang upside down to such an extent that their internal organs are located in a different arrangement than most other mammals of their size. Also, they sleep from 16 to 20 hours each day and their movements (when they do make them) are glacial. Sloths only leave their tree once a week to defecate and once a year to mate. Within this sedentary animal's fur lives a unique algae and within that algae lives a unique moth. Yes, that qualifies this animal as an oddity.

Interlopers: When Scott, Jenn, Darcy, Monica, Celia, and I went on our Costa Rica Adventure, we chose not to hire a sanctioned tour company to show  us around. You are warned by the cruise lines that these interlopers may cheat you and that their English speaking skills aren't that developed, but we had enough people in our group, that we weren't that concerned. We negotiated a fee for the entire day in an air conditioned van and went on our way. I have already explained the first part of our day that included the ferocious sounding howler monkey and our time in the banana plantations (Scott had asked Monica earlier "You wanna go on a banana adventure, of which she quickly agreed).

The second part of the day was shrouded by mystery with only a hint of possibilities when Darcy and Monica had said in sing/song voices "we want to see a three toed sloth." I had noticed the good looking owner of the van talking briefly on her cell phone a while before we drove into a backyard. We all sat with questioning looks as the driver shut off the van.

"We're here to see sloths," the owner said rolling her eyes, obviously bored.

Darcy with both sloths.

"Sloths, sloths, sloths!" Darcy and Monica joyfully screamed in unison and immediately became known by the rest of our group as "Sloth Whores"

A reasonably grungy man (interloper #2), who was presumably the owner of this rundown shanty, was climbing a tree in his backyard to pull down the three toed sloth that resided there. (He fed her to keep as a tourist magnet.) He handed her to the two girls and then pulled a three month old baby sloth from the mother's belly. He also showed the group cocoa nuts in various stages of development. Had we been interested, he would have sold us long hanging Montezuma Oriole

Monica with the baby sloth.

nests, which he had stolen from local palm trees. We all tipped the second interloper and continued on our way.

Tourists: As tourists on these *adventures* we are subject to roles of conduct of which we can't be proud. But hey, that sloth was something of an interloper herself, since she chose to stay there and be fed in exchange for being manhandled a few times each day.

Mind Musings in Turkey

Ideas must come from somewhere. Are they life creations (life being inscrutable) and we, as thoughtful individuals, just figure out ways to tune them in? Who knows?

Celia and I had just spent nearly an hour following our guide through the ancient ruins of Ephesus in western Turkey. We really had had no pre knowledge of this archeological site and were both impressed by the quality of the 2,600 year old ruins. Ephesus was the governmental center for dozens of cities and supposedly at one time had a population of nearly 200,000. The area of Ephesus that had so far been excavated represented only 15% of the entire city.

There was one set of information that our guide shared with us that intrigued me. A scientist/astronomer in Ephesus named Thele predicted that a total eclipse of the sun was to take place on a certain day and at a certain hour. The local authorities threatened him that if this event were not to take place when he predicted, that his life would be put in jeopardy—since he would be offending the gods. The day and hour came and the eclipse occurred as predicted, thus Thele was saved. In the ruins there is only a small portion of the original statue of Thele left (many earthquakes regularly hit in this area of the world)—it shows only one foot stepping on top of a sphere representing the earth. It would be nearly 2,100 years before Magellan would prove unequivocally that the earth was a sphere (rather than flat).

Thele's mind was attuned to truths—ideas that he was able to decipher. Which brings me to some research that was completed recently (and was discussed in the enigmatic movie, *A Waking Life*). A certain, somewhat difficult to solve, crossword puzzle was released to the public through the major newspapers on

Thele's foot with earth in front.

the east coast of the US. Researchers chose a random sampling of players and recorded the average time it took them to complete the puzzle. The same puzzle was then released a few days later to the major newspapers along the west coast of the US. Researchers once again recorded the average time of completion. Answers came decidedly quicker to the west coast puzzle solvers—implying that since the puzzles had already been solved a few days before—that their psychological fingerprint was drifting in a sort of global subconscious state— people were able to somehow 'tune in' to answers already solved. Interesting stuff. Just as Thele had, through his study, tuned into the correct date of the next solar eclipse and figured out proper shape of our Earth.

Egyptian Considerations

The dual nature of our wanderings through this life, both physical and psychological go hand in hand, sometimes make forming objective impressions difficult. This was true for Celia and my day in Egypt.

These multi-week cruises, although hardly disappointing on any level, border on (and sometimes cross that border) the mundane. Activities cater to middle class descriptors of fun and status—promoted diligently, and oftentimes shamelessly, by a staff of hundreds, in an effort to create an homogenized *good time* for the 1,800 people aboard our ship, and thus bring them back to cruising again and again.

At 7AM on a Sunday in December we were among this self-designated *convoy of elite* as 50 motor coaches left the port of Alexandria, Egypt (escorted by police cars) to travel the 150 or so miles to Giza (and the prize of visiting the pyramids). The first few miles curved through the city streets of the harbor area of Alexandria (10 million people) displaying meaningful evidence for what our guide described as "a third world country".

"Why would any of you wish to move to Egypt?" she said almost in her introductory comments, "The average income for most of the population of 73 million people is $360 a month—

we have two classes of people here in Egypt—the very rich and the very poor."

She made no statements about the dilapidated buildings, the trash strewn streets, or the gritty pollution that filled the air and covered everything with an orange layer (many of the few cars along the streets had covers over them), but she did comment on a beautiful shopping center we passed after leaving the congested port area and which obviously served the few who could afford it.

"This is what globalization wants for all of our country to be like. There is a TGI Fridays restaurant in that mall where one can spend 200 of their dollars for a family—for one meal! Can you imagine spending more than half of your monthly income on one meal!" Manal said, obviously not wishing to disguise her bias against the wealthy living in her country.

There weren't many cars on the expressway which linked the coast of the Mediterranean with the cities of Giza and Cairo (22 million people). About half of Egypt's population lives along this fertile Nile River corridor. There was farming of many crops along the way (Egypt is known for its cotton).

When we arrived at the pyramids we were given a mere 40 minutes to explore among the two largest pyramids and were warned *not* to pay the 20 Euros to walk inside the structures (dark, tight fitting, nothing to see was the reasoning) and also not to pay the vendors to have our photos taken on a camel (there was a small charge for getting on the camel—but also an unstated, higher charge to be taken off the camel). The vendors were once again as bothersome as the ones we encountered in Turkey—half of our time was taken trying to avoid the scams they presented (usually selling shoe shines or 10 postcards for one Euro). One group of vendors/beggars walked up to us with their hands out to shake ours, "Welcome to Egypt" they said with opened mouths and their two or three teeth showing. If we tried to resist their hands they would scream "You insult my family, not to shake my hand!" But when I did relent one time, the man wouldn't loosen his grip and began talking to me about his starving children and needing money. For a country whose number one industry is tourism, (The #2 industry is revenue from the Suez Canal.) one would think that government officials might attempt to shield their guests from these ill kept representatives and their scams. Our guide admitted that no one really knows how the pyramids were built.

"One very well respected researcher believes that each of the large pyramids were built in 20 years by tens of thousands of workers," she laughed, "more than three million, 12 to 20 ton blocks placed togeth-

er in 20 years."

That would be one block set in place every two minutes— for more than 7,000 straight days. Why do people pretend to know about the pyra-

mids? They are a mystery; and always will be a mystery.

We also visited the Sphinx, the step pyramid, the statues at Memphis, and had lunch at a luxury hotel near the pyramids that appeared, as an oasis, among the squalor (and was very well guarded).

We arrived back at the ship by 8 PM (which sailed two hours later). It will probably be a few months for a more substantiated and thoughtful opinion of this day in Egypt to set in my mind.

Things Natural

In the D. H. Lawrence travelogue about Italy, he included 115 pages about the Etruscans. He visited the area northwest of Rome where no ruins of the Etruscans 6th century B.C. existence could be found (since they built primarily with wood) but a couple dozen (of the thousands known to exist) intricate, wall painted Etruscan tombs were accessible to the paying tourists. What Lawrence found, and how he described this discovery, I found to be some of the most intriguing and well written literature I have yet to read.

What Lawrence attempts to pinpoint is the act of being *natural*. His interpretations of the colorful paintings found in the many tombs he explored relate an aboriginal lifestyle based upon the gifts that life offers us.

Naked, painted (in red) hunters celebrating the art of natural living. Of course, when the Roman Empire discovered these people it reacted similarly as our ancestors did when they discovered the aboriginal people of the Americas (the Indians)—they wiped them out. The Romans described them as 'vicious people' and backward—thus they needed to be eliminated.

This reading makes me consider what is *natural* in our lives. It is easy this time of year to make considerations, as millions of people gather worldwide to bring in the year 2010, one of the innumerable *rites of passage* that define our planet's yearly revolution around the sun. We will now wait for MLK Day, Valentine's Day, St. Patrick's Day, Easter, Cinco de Mayo, Memorial Day, Fourth of July, Labor Day, Halloween, Thanksgiving, and once again Christmas and New Years.

Along with these time honored holiday traditions in our country: birthdays, anniversaries, and sporting events also serve to distract notions of a natural life—NFL Playoffs, Super Bowl, NHL and NBA championships, MLB; 162 game seasons keeps six months of interest, plus the playoffs and World Series.

Basically, if one also delves into the daily senseless, continual political intrigues (television and radio's news creating, talking heads) that spout our way—there is little time during our 365 days for self-consideration. I think that we should all consider a more natural life. The word natural simply means living closer to nature. How natural is our lives?

I consider a tuft of grass I saw recently that held three beautiful yellow flowers. This grassy area served as a border between a forested area and the huge Sahara Desert. It also looked upon the pyramids. This first week of December spotlighted the peak of the flower's existence. Their flowering perfection out-shined the three decaying geometric structures and the Sphinx millions of people flocked to see.

Also, if one considers the natural state of this image, in a million years, these structures will have worn away and the flowers will still be blooming during the first weeks of December. Their naturalness is infinite. There is little natural about the things that people make.

We enter this life naked and innocent and reach our physical peak somewhere around the age of 35. Yet, we are also given the gift of time consciousness, which allows us the opportunity to offer a sense of the natural in each day of our lives. This sense must embrace gentleness and kindness. By passing these powerful feelings on to our offspring and the people we claim as friends, we, like the gentle yellow flowers in Egypt can claim an eternal domain.

Nothin Left to Lose

"Freedom's just another word for *nothin' left to lose.*" This lyric from Kris Kristofferson's song, *Me and Bobby McGee* has bounced through my mind for nearly four decades maybe because I saw Janis Joplin sing it at a concert in Wisconsin somewhere around 1969. Those nine words in the song never made much sense to

 me—until recently.

I found myself in an informal line—waiting to use a single unisex bathroom on a rural Tuscany (actually Lazio) olive tree farm—about 90 miles from Rome. Celia and I had chosen this low impact excursion rather than to involve ourselves in the hectic business of being a part of the throng in downtown Rome. Four huge tour buses had each taken 40 people each to four separate farm settings. A narrow, windy, non-shouldered road barely allowed our bus to stay between the lines. Our farm was the smallest and oldest of the four (around 10 acres—and the olive trees were centuries old).

We were taken through vegetable gardens, given wine and goat cheese, and breads dipped in their extra virgin olive oil. We also saw in the distance among the crop rows a 300-year-old oak tree that had a tree house built in its branches—this farm was also a bed and breakfast and the tree house was an option for the guests.

There were two cordial Italian owners who (in broken English) told us that they rarely visited the nearest town and grew nearly all of the food that they needed. This had to be one of the most scenic and idyllic locations Celia and I had ever visited.

It was within this reality that a taller, loud spoken man walked up to get into line. "What do you think of this place, Illinois?" he asked. (I was wearing a University of Illinois sweatshirt.)

"Really beautiful and peaceful." I responded, not really wanting a conversation with this man, who had early on revealed himself to be a boor. (I mentally willed that whomever now occupied the bathroom would open the door and save me).

"Not me! I'd go nuts out here in the middle of nowhere! I'd have to put an airstrip in, build a bunch of condo's, and make some money off this place—but, I could never live out here! That's just who I am. I sell real estate." *Surprise, surprise* I thought (he never looked me in the eye). The bathroom door opened and I escaped without having to respond.

This man had much to lose by living out here—his ambition, lack of individual imagination, and ego prevented him from seeing the true beauty being bestowed. This place seemed nothing less than a paradise for Celia and me.

By giving up one's ego and (its sidekick) short-sightedness—one indeed becomes *free* and can thus have nothin' left to lose.

A Narrow Strip of Sand

A great frigate bird glided effortlessly above the beach where Celia and I were reclined—enjoying the hot Caribbean sun. We were relaxing at a beach that was part of a club. In order to join this club a person must invest $100,000. For this investment, the new club member receives access to one of nearly 100, two bedroom units for three weeks out of the year. The member wouldn't own a specific unit and the weeks assigned would have to change from year to year so that other members would be able to book the more popular weeks. Along with this initial investment the new members were responsible for a yearly maintenance fee of $20,000.

Celia and I were on this beach because our son is a manager at this club, and we were killing time before returning to our cruise ship. But, Celia and I weren't worried about the other people on the beach realizing that they were amongst two interlopers—since of the dozen or so couples and small families around us (whom our frigate bird was also looking down upon) none seemed to give any of the others the time of day. Most had sculpted, perfectly tanned bodies and were talking on cell phones.

This struck me as a very expensive club to be practicing an isolationist policy. I inwardly wondered if our majestic frigate bird (sort of a high flying keeper of these Caribbean Islands) had any sort of consciousness beyond its drive to eat and reproduce—and if it did I am sure that it would give a curious look to this expensive, non social club.

I looked down at the book I had been reading for the past month; a book of critical essays on the writer D. H. Lawrence. I was re-reading an essay on the poems Lawrence had written and I had to smile at the poignancy of the poem highlighted in this essay:

Wages

The wages of work is cash. The wages of cash is want of more cash. The wages of want of more cash is vicious competition. The wages of vicious competition is the world we live in. The work-cash-want circle is the viciousest circle that ever turned men into fiends. Earning a wage is a prison occupation and a wage earner is a sort of jail bird. Earning a salary is a prison overseers job—a jailer instead of a jail bird. Living on your income is strolling grandly outside the prison in terror, lest you have to go in. And since the work-prison covers almost every scrap of the living earth, you stroll up and down on a narrow beat, about the same as a prisoner taking their exercise. This is called universal freedom.

I looked up from my book and wondered what the violently independent minded Lawrence might think of what our society has become in the 76 years since his passing? I feel fairly certain that he would look at all of the technical advances in communications as a means to better define our prison society. The *narrow beat* of freedom we walked at the beginning of the twentieth century has gotten quite a bit more narrow.

So I looked around the beach and saw my capitalistic beach

sharers strolling on their narrow strip of sand—ignoring each other and the non-solid bars that make up their personal prison club—as my frigate bird disappeared over a ridge to explore a new beach.

A Victory for Testosterone

I agreed to go on this 12-day transatlantic cruise with five females. I believe that most of my male friends would agree that I had set myself up for a reasonable amount of misery—for, no matter how cordial and entertaining these women could be, the fact still remains, that chemically speaking, their views of reality simply are not on the same dimensional plane as a man's.

Although the entire experience was quite enjoyable, I was in a constant state of apprehension. Let's face it, women think differ-

ently. Allow me to give you an example of a small success story that I attained on this trip.

One of the five females had been to the Portuguese island of which we had just docked. There was a tram that took tourists to a mountain top on this side of the island. Once off of this tram, one could pay $25 for two people and have two young Portuguese men slide you halfway down the steep narrow streets, in a wooden basket, on runners (which they greased). You would then walk the last three kilometers or so back toward the ship.

I had agreed to accompany the five, but had a plan not to get into the basket and tell them that I would walk down. Well, once the five began getting into the baskets, one of them suggested that I walk ahead, so that they would slide by me. I had planned to wave goodbye and then get back on the tram and head down. So now, I was walking down a nearly 45 degree angled street, but seeing taxis going by asking if I wanted a ride. I smiled to myself.

Here came three of the girls in their baskets with their Portu-guese boy toys. One of the most rambunctious of the three was scream-ing, spin it, spin it."

I jumped toward the wall and acted like they were going to hit me. They screamed as their baskets zoomed by me. It didn't seem to me that they were going that fast; now, if they would have had wheels.

Next came the second basket with the other two...this basket seemed to be traveling even slower. What a racket. A ten minute ride for 25 bucks. Young Portuguese men have probably been do-ing this for decades. I once again acted like I was going to be hit. The female units seemed to enjoy this reaction.

Once both baskets were out of sight, I flagged down a taxi and had the driver take me to the town area, where I relaxed, bought some unbelievably tasty tangerines, and then hiked back to the ship.

The girl's waited 45 minutes for me, concerned that I had fallen

The girls looking for me.

or something. I told them that I had asked the taxi driver to take me to the end of your run, but he hadn't understood. But later, I let slip the fact that he told me that taxi drivers on this island have to change their brakes every two months.

It was great fun ditching them. I am sure I will pay for this indiscretion for a long time. But, it was a small victory for testosterone.

Ice Cream Wars

To experience a cruise aboard the luxury liners around the world oftentimes is a sensory overload. It's simply a lot, for someone wishing to report on all of the nuances, to take in. Yes, cruising is, for those of us whom find pleasure in viewing the terrain of the humans, a spectator sport.

I've found some of the best locations for this viewing aboard these giant ships is generally wherever people must gather for the consumption of food. I'm not talking about the evening meals— I'm talking about the large buffets that generally exist on one of the top decks, usually on the same deck as the swimming pools.

I'm rarely disappointed when I go to these places. I immediately think about the time when our family had two dogs at our home in Alaska. I would put food out on our deck for both of them to eat. Freckles was the dominant dog. If he was around, Boots the sub dominant dog wouldn't approach the food. But if Freckles was eating the food and Boots would happen to get too near to him, Freckles would emit a low bare-toothed growl and Boots would immediately whimper away.

I believe that I've discovered a food area that consistently displays to we spectators the human version of a bare-toothed growl—this being the ice cream counter. The specifics of this ice cream counter add to the joy of watching. It is only about 10 feet across. It has a soft ice cream machine at one side, around eight choices of hard packed ice cream, and then it has five clear plastic cylinders holding both peanut and regular M and Ms, Gummy Worms, Reese's Pieces, and Jelly Beans. Add to this, that it is only opened for six hours each day.

Doesn't this look like a safe venue? Allow me to describe an event Celia, Missy, Will, and I witnessed a few days ago. I had filled my plate with a late afternoon snack of a cheeseburger and fries and found a seat close to the ice cream stand.

"Howie—when are you going to grow some hair and stand up to Sal? "

I heard this rude comment coming from behind me and turned to get a visual perspective. I saw this large woman with shortly cropped dark hair leaning across the table berating her meek acting husband. He had to be her husband, because is forehead was slanted in such a submissive manner, proving that he had endured the brunt of this female dominatrix for decades. As if having eyes in the back of her head, she turned and stared at me as I was assessing this henpecking terrain. Her glaring eyes frightened me, but, I was saved, I believe from any caustic remarks headed my way, by the fact that Celia, Will, and Missy were now joining me at the table. I began talking with my friends, but still kept an ear directed toward the poor drone Howie, whose queen bee kept up her verbal attack.

"I'm going up to get some ice cream!" Howie's nightmarish bride announced and got up. "Howie, don't let the waiter take my coffee!" The probable 1950 Miss New Jersey candidate whom had undoubtably come in last place in the congeniality competition, further yelled back when she had walked just past our table, defining her domineering nature and giving me a second glance. I shuttered. I wanted to lean back and tell Howie to make a run for it.

Now, the ice cream stand became Act Two. I motioned for my fellow table-mates to pay attention. The fact that the ice cream stand has no sign indicating in which direction people should line up represents the cause of about 80% of the dramas.

When our female Godzilla initially headed toward the ice cream stand, there was nobody waiting, but as she had stopped and made her loud announcement about the coffee to Howie, three people suddenly appeared seeking the sugary delights.

A late seventies lady beat out our New Jersey nemesis, with another similar-aged couple being behind her and seeming not too happy at being in third place.

"What kinds of ice cream do you have?" the first lady asked.

"Flavors listed in front ma'am," Sergie from Croatia answered.

"Okay, I'll have a cone of chocolate," she finally decided after hearing a loud sigh from our heroine behind her. "Wait." she said. "Could I change that to a hard packed dish?"

It was at least two minutes of haggling with a frustrated Sergie and getting both types of M and Ms, plus some Gummy Worms added before the near Alzheimer poster girl completed her order. At one point in this confusing transaction, when the older lady asked to replace a yellow gummy worm with a green one, our protagonist emitted a string of mule skinner words loud enough for all to hear. Also, at the same time, the couple behind Miss New Jersey moved to the left side of the stand and pretended to form a new line. Two others were now in line behind them on the left hand side. When the older woman finally left the booth with her chocolate ice cream covered with green Gummy Worms, the lady and her husband on the left tried to place an order.

"Excuse me!" our heroine responded in disbelief! "Listen lady. I was in front of you!"

"The line forms behind me," the lady stated seeming unimpressed by the bully.

"Unless you want to wear your ice cream, you better back off lady."

The woman gave out a big sigh and announced, "Sergie, you decide who's first in line?" she pointed at a frightened Sergie.

Sergie's eyes got big and didn't respond. Finally, our queen bee stated "Sergie, I want two scoop of chocolate ice cream with chocolate syrup on top."

The woman on the left pointed at our New Jerseyite's middle and said, "I think you need the ice cream more than I do. Come on Walter, we're leaving."

"Madam. Don't leave," we heard Sergie say.

"Let the bitch go!" our lady stated triumphantly and brought her dish of ice cream past us stopping and announcing, "Have you ever wanted to shove ice cream right into someone's face?" she asked the four of us and we all laughed at her—happy at now being an ally of hers—we still had six more days onboard. That was a good thing.

I smiled.

And Then Again

On a cold, snowy night in Cambridge, Massachusetts, an auditorium on Harvard School of Law's campus was filled to capacity. It was December 10, 1973, (Celia and I had been married a little more than two weeks.) and most of the law students who packed this room would readily admit that although many of them had read some of the writings of tonight's speaker, they came out of curiosity, for to understand the arcane, scientific direction of R. Buckminster Fuller's writings was outside of most people's comprehension—especially pre-law students. The students applauded as a bald, lithe man of seventy-nine years strode confidently up to the microphone. He seemed to pay little attention to their act of affirmation, and I wondered if he came here (he had spoken at Harvard several times before) to psychologically slap the face of the institution that had twice thrown him out as a student, for raucous behavior. He began to speak, and for the next hour and a half he spoke quickly—what he called 'thinking aloud.' He spoke of his life as a futurist and as an inventor from his birth in 1895 until this moment.

I own a cassette recording of this speech and occasionally listen to it order to refresh my spirit. When this speech occurred, our country was on the verge of having it's first president resign. We were ending the Viet Nam War and the lives of more than

50,000 young soldiers had been lost in the name of 'freedom.' Now, as I write these words, nearly thirty years later, our country is once again becoming involved in a conflict on the other side of our globe. This time using advanced weaponry of all kinds—and once again, all in the name of *freedom*.

Mr. Fuller's focus of conversation that chilly evening was on the possibility of mankind being able to generate the same energy and finances that is being expended upon weaponry onto peaceful strategies for the development of livingry. His take upon the world political was that the technological and agricultural advances made in the previous 100 years now made it possible for all of the five billion people on our planet (in 1973) to have enough food to eat and to live in a safe and clean environment. What prevents this from happening is the existence of nearly 200 governments that have sectioned off the lands and the waters into possessive, nationalistic, patriotic zones.

Mr. Fuller makes the case that all of these governments have such greedy self interests that the well being of it's populace is a secondary issue to the *thugs* who have, in various dark, unpublicized ways garnered power and now need to protect their own personal agendas. He talked of the savagery of war and how no matter how governments or individuals attempt to justify battle field deaths along patriotic, ideologic, theologic, or moralistic grounds, it really is simply murder. We train people to murder other people, and if they do it on their own they go to prison. If they do it for their country they get medals.

Mr. Fuller, who always loved using large words and sentences, used the following terminology to describe how he believed the world would eventually find its way out of the present political, military, and economic maze that confounded his 1973 world. He was candid in his feeling that the world was several hundred years from this escape.

From Earth, Inc.
by R. Buckminster Fuller 1973
What I am trying to do

Acutely aware of our beings' limitations and acknowledging the infinite mystery of the a priori Universe into which we are born but nevertheless searching for a conscience means of hopefully competent participation by humanity in its own evolutionary trending while employing only the unique advantages inhering exclusively to those individuals who take and maintain the economic initiative in the face of the formidable physical capital and credit advantages of the massive corporations and political states and deliberately avoiding politicalties and tactics while endeavoring by experiments and explorations to excite individuals' awareness and realization of humanity's higher potentials

I seek through comprehensive anticipatory design science and its reductions to physical practices to reform the environment instead of trying to reform humans, being intent thereby to accomplish prototyped capabilities of doing more with less whereby in turn the wealth augmenting prospects of such design science regenerations will induce their spontaneous and economically successful industrial proliferation by world around services' managements all of which chain reaction provoking events will both permit and induce all humanity to realize full lasting economic and physical success plus enjoyment of all the Earth without one individual interfering with or being advantaged at the expense of another.

R. Buckminster Fuller
Comprehensive Anticipatory Design Science

What this means is that when you change an environment, you change attitudes. As a 26-year veteran of elementary classrooms I used this concept from the beginning of my career. Whenever I was unfortunate enough to inherit an unruly group of students, I would change bulletin boards, seating arrangements, teaching strategies, and reward systems sometimes as often as weekly. Such an uncertain and constantly changing environment kept these classes motivated and behavior was rarely an issue.

Mr. Fuller's invention of the geodesic dome and his promotion to city planners of urban models of efficiency and beauty were his hope for mankind. But there was one section on the ancient cassette tape that motivated me to write this essay. He stated in a slower speech cadence than the rest of his speech that:

> "The world should begin to support each person's right to maintain his or her human dignity... it shouldn't matter if a billionaire or a beggar stands before you... they both possess beautiful souls... their lives, as is each of the lives of all of us in this auditorium is a Pulitzer prize winning novel waiting to be written by an author who knows what truth really is. If a person has more money than another, does that make him a better person? Most very wealthy people I have known are incredible bores (laughter). There are presently five billion people on our Spaceship Earth and each of those people should be a billionaire..."

There was a long pause on the cassette tape as I listened. "Did everyone in here hear me? "the little man with the large glasses said again. Then he raised his voice for the only time in this hour and a half presentation.

"Everyone on this planet should be a billionaire"

R. Buckminster Fuller was in the Navy in the 1920s and prided himself in evaluating the efficiency of systems and machines based upon his military experience. Knowing a ship's gross weight, displacement, and speed based upon drag coefficients and extremes in environmental conditions were systems that interested Mr. Fuller. By using this background of knowledge, he set out to analyze livingry systems.

Buckminster Fuller passed away in 1983 before he could witness a trend on our Spaceship Earth (as he called it) that would embrace his concept of Anticipatory Design Science. Ironically, this trend has its genesis upon the same oceans that spawned many of Fuller's philosophies. I had an opportunity in 1982 to fly from Tyonek to Anchorage and hear him speak, but weather prevented it. Although in 1969 I did hitchhike from Bloomington, Illinois down to Carbondale, where Fuller was a lecturing professor for many years on Southern Illinois' campus, to listen to several of Bucky's audio-tapes, and where I acquired the tape I am now writing about.

This positive, oceanic creative force is the cruise line industry. On a recent ten day cruise Celia and I took out of Miami, a thumbnail analysis might serve as an appropriate example for supporting my supposition.

The ship we were aboard weighed 85,000 tons and has a capacity of nearly 3,000 passengers and crew. It travels at an average of 18 knots and has stabilizers that make only the roughest seas physical inconvenience for its passengers. This ship is in use virtually every week of the year either in the Caribbean or in Europe. So, it services nearly 100,000 passengers a year. The science of people management upon this ship is truly fine tuned, with enough daily activities and varieties of quality foods to make every person on board feel like a billionaire.

How do I view an industry that most people feel is beyond their economic capacity as an area that could lead us from our patriotically saturated warring mentality?

After taking a look at the basic statistics of this vehicle, which so precisely carries this mass of crew and passengers, let's view the passengers themselves. The ship had 2,100 passengers. There were people representing 54 different countries (I asked the purser). Nearly every race and main religion of mankind were also represented. The age spectrum stretched from a one year old girl to a man of 92 years of age. Political beliefs of every governmental device held passions variable.

All of the human elements of diversity existed upon this ship that might lead emotional conflicts (especially since a globally unpopular war was taking place during the voyage) but of course, nothing remotely in the strain of political controversy took place.

Nothing happened because as Buckminster Fuller might say 'the family of mankind's similarities were being addressed, rather than their differences.' These 2,100 people were being treated as royalty; delicious food of every possible variety were offered, activities that encouraged conversations amongst strangers, and an obsequious and incredibly cordial crew made the individual's every need a priority-basically Fuller's dream 'that all aboard this beautiful planet should be treated as billionaires' was being played out for these ten days.

I can see Bucky's immensely analytic brain at work had he been able to view the facts of this industry. In the year 2000, nine million people cruised the world's oceans and seas (13 million in 2009). They were aboard more than 500 luxury ships. Fuller would view these 500 ships as 500 separate globally independent governments traveling outside the jurisdictions of the self-serving gang mentality, that the world's leaders now possess-as patriotic manipulators-who also happily sculpt (with the help of a paid off media) their populace into fear reacting members who will gladly support their leadership with ever increasing tax dollars, so that *their gang* will be the most powerful on the planet.

No gangs aboard this ship.

Fuller would create charts showing how the promotion of this *positive industry* of cruising could lead from 500 ships in 2000 to 5,000 ships by 2050 and 10,000 ships by 2100. With these 10,000 ships carrying 30 million passengers a week and zero population growth being attained (that put our peak population at 12 billion inhabitants) it should then be possible that every person 18 years and older could take a *peace cruise* at least once every five years. A portion of everyone's employment checks could be taken out to support this peace sustaining concept.

War would become obsolete, as our similarities are celebrated. Buckminster Fuller would then be smiling somewhere, as he views this hopeful hypothesis. It might be that this notion over-simplifies possibilities—but then again maybe it doesn't.

7235508R0

Made in the USA
Charleston, SC
07 February 2011